THE CRATER OF ORIZABA
and other stories

by
BART BONNER

Underground Voices
Los Angeles, California
2016

Published by Underground Voices
www.undergroundvoices.com
Editor contact: Cetywa Powell

ISBN Number: 978-0990433194
Printed in the United States of America.

Cover image from a lithograph entitled "L'ORIZABA" by
Eugene Ciceri (1813-1890)
Printed by Lemercier & Co., Paris, circa 1875

TABLE OF CONTENTS

THE CRATER OF ORIZABA
and other stories

Preface

The stories in this collection are organized by region. A few of the stories that unfold in the southern part of the world ("Maori Land" and "The Portenian" come to mind) seemed to have surfaced of their own accord, with little aforethought, as though having long laid dormant, waiting for a medium to release them to the page. These stories arrived spontaneously; one might even say, without exaggeration, by way of catharsis. Other stories emerged more deliberately, through the slow, methodical faceting of ideas, taking shape more by hammer and chisel than by transcription. Each is a journey of discovery in its own right; and regardless of the method employed, there is always an unwavering focus on the craft of writing. More than once have I walked away from a story astonished by the impact that a single word substitution can have on a story's power to produce an emotional connection with the reader: my respect for the process of editing knows no bounds.

While no common thread binds these stories together, the reader may nevertheless find a clustering of themes within the regional boundaries under which these stories are categorized, as well as cross-culturally where common behaviors transcend our physical and psychological demarcations. The reader will encounter, for example, characters driven by the struggle for wealth — that singular impulse that so dramatically defines our history, resulting in abnormal risk-taking, clashes between the local and the outsider, and offensive machinations of orchestrated deceit.

Aside from the eternal struggle to improve one's lot in life, one might encounter other themes within this volume: themes of loss and sacrifice; of man against nature; and of explorations into the ephemeral nature of identity. Five of the stories in this collection take the reader on journeys at extreme elevations, exploring man's struggles with himself, with his companions, and with an unforgiving environment where the air is thin and judgment is susceptible to impairment. Several of these stories explore conflicts and confrontations between individuals struggling to understand their place in the world. Four stories explore the consequences of living in a totalitarian state, where the trajectories of life are subject to institutional bending and distortion. There are stories, too, populated with characters that scheme, conspire, plot, and knock loudly on our door, demanding to be heard, insisting on staking their claim to the bounty they feel is their rightful inheritance. Discovering what they have to say, and guarding oneself against falling victim to their trickery, is, I hope, a challenge worth taking for the reader.

Stories in this collection have been published in the following print literary reviews, in order of publication date.

Acknowledgements

"Maori Land", *Chaminade Literary Review (US)*, 1995

"The Portenian", originally published as "A Day In San Telmo" by *Mind in Motion (US)*, 1995, revision printed by *Matter Journal (US)*, Issue 9, 2007

"The Crater of Orizaba", *South Dakota Review (US)*, 2007

"The Voice of Silvia", *Buenos Aires Literary Review (ARG)*, 2007. Story published in North America by *Matter Journal, Issue 10 (US), 2007*.

"A Chance Meeting At Luigi's Café", *Existere – Journal of Arts and Literature, (CA)*, 2007

"The One That Got Away", *Matter Journal, Issue 11 (US)*, 2008

"Loughlin's Trade", *Matter Journal, Issue 8* (US), 2006

"The Water Wheel", *Takahe (NZ)*, 2009

"Los Penitentes", *The MacGuffin (US)*, 2009

"Rule 21," *Words and Images (US)*, 2009

"The Lagerstatten", *You Are Here (US)*, 2009

"Tapu", *The Wanderlust Review (US)*, 2010

"Jameson's Letters", *Voice From The Planet (US)*, Harvard Square Edition Anthology, 2010

"The Human Cry", *Tidal Basin Review (US)*, 2010

"The Accelerated Man", *The Delinquent (UK), 2011*

"El Nevado de Cachi", *American Anethaeum,* 2012

"Bay of Bengal", *The Sand Canyon Review* (US), 2013

I. ARGENTINA

The Voice of Silvia

Our bus pulls into the village of El Bolson and creaks to a halt by a sign outside a closed grocery store. "We leave at seven-thirty," the driver says, rubbing his gloved hands, his words a fog in the mountain air. "Don't be late."

I disembark, leaving my bags stowed underneath, to visit the snow-covered streets and find a place to eat. The air is frigid, pure, scented with pine; as I throw my head back to look at the sky I see enormous snow crystals falling in a slow-motion dance, melding together as though in conjugal embrace, anointing my shoulders. I blow into my hands, survey the gray Andean horizon, and am awed by the line of jagged peaks thrusting heavenward, blanketed in a mantle of pristine whiteness. The local landmark, *Piltriquitron*, rises majestically into an ominous mass of dark cloud; at its base the outline of an alluvial fan spreads like a flattened pyramid into the cold, Patagonian valley, disintegrating and stripping the barren slopes of their crumbling granitic outcrops with slow, imperceptible movements.

My boots crunch the virgin snow as I trod down the main road towards the cluster of buildings where lights can be seen through the curtained windows. On the way I meet a few old gauchos, dressed in black berets and heavy woolen coats, clipping along on their nags, speaking in rural colloquialisms and puffing on hand-rolled cigarettes. "*Buenas tardes*," they say, touching their berets. "*Caballeros*," I reply, nodding politely. They smile, having figured me immediately for one of the Porteños who occasionally pass through their village on their way to Esquel or Bariloche.

I find a small, one room restaurant — called, simply, "La Parrilla" — run by a squat, gray-haired woman who speaks a heavily accented, yet understandable, Castilian. The walls and ceiling are made of logs, as are many of the buildings in the valley, but the place looks clean and well kept. A fire crackles and throws sparks on one side of the room, which is illuminated, in its darker corners, by the dull yellow glows of lamp wicks. Over the mantle-piece hangs a watercolor painting of the Argentine flag, and next to it, a black and white framed photo of our president, Juan Peron. In one of the corners stands a bar, hardly bigger in size than a lectern, with a shelf on the wall lined with bottles of various shapes and sizes. A few *paisanos* are huddled there, their whiskered faces illuminated by a kerosene lamp. They cast sidelong glances at me as I enter, then, sensing me harmless, return to their cane liquor and their whispered conversations.

I order a cup of coffee and a beefsteak, and take a seat at a wobbly table aside two men playing cards.

"Silvia," the proprietress calls.

A girl appears. She is maybe nineteen, twenty years old, tall, not particularly pretty, but finely featured and eerily attractive. She begins to converse with the proprietress in a soothing, hypnotic, sing-song voice, and immediately the patrons sitting at the tables around me, standing by the warmth of the fire, most of them bus passengers like myself, grow quiet, and turn their heads to glare at her. Listening to them speak, I am struck by a stark dichotomy of sound, by an arresting contrast between the elder woman's harsh, guttural consonants and the soft, youthful phrases that Silvia chooses to express herself.

She stands with great poise. She gesticulates with her hands. A strand of dark hair covers her face. She smiles, brushes the hair away. She then nods to the older woman and heads back into the kitchen, completely unaware of the attention fixated on her.

The room is quiet. The fire crackles. Someone coughs.

Finally I hear a chair scrape the floor and I see a small but stocky mustachioed man with a retrousse nose approach the counter. Smoothing his moustache with his index finger, he says: "Excuse me. I couldn't help overhearing that girl who was speaking to you a moment ago. She has a wonderful voice. Would you permit her to sit at my table for an hour or so? I wish to listen to her speech."

The woman throws an offended look at the patron. "What do you think this is," she snaps. "A bordello?"

"No. I mean nothing disrespectful, I assure you. It's simply that I want to listen to her voice. Look, I'll pay you ten pesos."

The proprietress, lost in thought, wipes the counter with a rag. She looks up at her customer with suspicion. "Make it thirty and I'll allow it," she says, as though doubting her counteroffer would be accepted.

"Very well," the man agrees. He digs into his wallet and withdraws three ten peso notes. "Here. I'll give you ten now, and the rest later."

"No. I'll have twenty now, and ten later."

The man nods impatiently. He hands her the notes. The old woman grins as she stuffs the bills in her sweater pocket.

"Silvia," she calls. "Come here."

The girl appears. Her hair is stringy and unwashed. Her teeth are crooked. Her eyes, however, shine with watery luminosity and embrace you tenderly as she speaks with that harp-like voice, in those innocent, silken tones that so allure and transfix the listener by virtue of their sweet and sensual vibrations.

"Listen," says the proprietress. "I'll take over in the kitchen. I want you to go sit down over there with that man and talk to him. He's passing through and wants some company."

The girl, Silvia, folds her hands inside a dishcloth and glances nervously at the man. "I don't know," she says. "What if I don't like him?"

"Oh, you'll like him all right," the woman assures her. "You'll like him or I'll put you back on that bus to Esquel. It may interest you to know that that cretin husband of yours was in here the other day demanding to know your whereabouts."

Silvia's face grows dark as she backs out of the lamplight. "You're always saying that when you want me to do something you know I wouldn't consent to voluntarily!"

"It's true. He knows you work here."

"Did you tell him?"

"No. But do as I say, and the next time he comes I'll tell him that I had to let you go."

"I'm not an escort service," Silvia protests.

The man with the moustache gets up from his chair and makes his way over to the counter. The other patrons, having witnessed the arrangement between him and the proprietress, are now watching and listening.

"Pardon," he says. "I hope I didn't offend you, miss. My name is Dr. Julio Alvarez. I'm a linguistics professor in Neuquen. I teach French, Italian, Portuguese, English, Latin, and German; and I study and lecture and write books on phonology. All my life I've been fascinated by the human voice. I'm joined in this appreciation by a small group of academics and religious scholars who realize that in rare cases the human voice, as if by some random mutation, is transformed into an instrument of divinity; that at any given point in time there are certain individuals — maybe no more than a dozen the world over — whose voices become conduits for the whispers of the Almighty. Usually these individuals are unaware of their own gift, unaware that their speech conveys a curing effect that has been described as miraculous. In Medieval times these gifted persons were burned at the stake as witches, while in Africa and other regions of the world they were exalted as gods and shamans. I know all this because for centuries our group has studied and maintained a registry of all the known

"Sirens of God", as they are sometimes called, though some find this characterization misleading, even offensive. There has not been an addition to this registry since 1932, the last being a young woman from Clairvaux, France whose voice was so angelic that she was reported to have healed the cancers of four of her fellow villagers as they lay withering away on their death beds. In short, miss, knowing as we do the Siren's unique linguistic signature, I am certain that you are one of these very special individuals, whose voice is not only beautiful to the ear, but also intrinsically divine. That is why I wish to listen to you speak."

Silvia lets out a gasp and immediately covers her mouth as if she had suddenly lost control of her voice. She is staring now at Dr. Alvarez, who is staring back at her, awaiting a reply. Beside her stands the old woman, locked in a stony silence, open-mouthed and incredulous.

A man by the fireplace breaks in: "I didn't understand a single word of what that man just said, but the girl does have a pleasant voice and I'd like to hear her speak too. I can't pay what he did, but I'll serve up a round of *mate* to her and to anybody else who will listen." He holds up the teakettle that he had previously hung over the fire on a metal spit.

Silvia turns on the proprietress. "So. This man paid you. You didn't tell me that. How much did he give you?"

"I gave her twenty pesos," Alvarez interrupts, "to compensate her for the lost labor. I'll pay you another ten when the hour's up."

"No!" the old woman objects. "You pay me that other ten, not her."

"*Epá!*" says one of the card players. "The old lady drives a hard bargain, eh, Juan?" This comment is addressed in a loud voice to his *truco* partner, who sits across the table, glaring at his cards in silence. "Perhaps the twenty should go to the girl," he continues, "and the ten should go to the old lady when she's done." The card player winks judiciously at his partner, who merely frowns.

"Yes," says an old man, raising his cane as if to second the motion. "I agree with him. It's not fair that the girl gets the short end of it." He displays his solidarity with the *truco* player by holding out the brass handle of his cane in a sort of papal gesture, after which he gives little authoritative nods at the patrons who glance his way.

"Look," the old woman protests. "I run this place, and I give the orders around here. However, out of respect for your patronage and sense of justice, I'll let her keep the ten pesos when she's done. No more than that!" She glares around the room defiantly. No one else objects. "All right then," she says. "The arrangement is made."

"Why don't you let her read something to us," suggests the man by the fireplace. "That way we can all hear her voice."

"Yes," the old man bellows. "Let the girl with the angelic voice read. Who knows? Maybe it will help prolong the life of an old man!"

"I left a book on the bus," I remark. "I'll go and get it, if you like."

Everyone agrees. So I go to fetch the book from the back seat of the decrepit bus. When I return, I wave Silvia over to the fireplace. "I hope you will excuse us," I say, "for imposing on you in this way." I retrieve a ten peso note from my pocket and slide it into the book, which I hand to her. She takes the book and grips it tightly to her chest. She then gazes at me with those big blue eyes and I suddenly have a vision of myself taking her in my arms at this moment and raining kisses on her neck. She is even more attractive up close, yet at the same time more repulsive as well — a dichotomy that I find difficult to reconcile. She looks at me and shivers: whether with pleasure or disgust or chill, I do not know. The room grows quiet. The patrons are watching her now. She opens the book and begins to read.

Her voice never once trembles, never falters or hesitates. We sit transfixed and motionless, as though posing for an artist, and listen in rapture to the cadence of her voice, rising and falling in sweet, soothing rhythm, her pronunciation impeccable, her elocution and delivery masterful. Her eyes never leave the pages but once, when she is handed the *mate* gourd by the man with the kettle. As she sips the hot green tea through the metal straw, she allows her eyes to wander about the room, to fall upon each face in her audience and swallow them with her glance. It is evident that her timidity has completely vanished, that she now knows that her voice is powerful and unique, and is amazed and even startled at the profound spell it casts on us. She continues to read, each word a caress, each sentence a strange, intangible massage to our inebriated minds; and when she finishes we sit quietly for several minutes, until, one by one, we stand up and wander over to shake her hand and congratulate her.

Our driver puts his head in the door. "We depart in five minutes."

As Silvia heads back toward the kitchen I take her by the arm: I am about to tell her that I will return one day, that I want to see her again; but I realize how absurd such statements will sound. I thank her instead, kiss her cold, ruddy cheek, and walk out the door of La Parrilla into the frigid night air.

As we pile into the bus we notice the swerving headlights of an approaching car, its engine rasping as it accelerates down the main road. The car slides to a halt in front of the lighted buildings. A man gets out, slams the car door shut with an alarming violence; his large frame, wrapped in a bulky coat and scarf, bends into the wind and snow as he strides into the restaurant. A moment later the door bursts open again, smashing loudly against the wall. I stand by the bus, waiting to board, watching this scene with a foreboding realization of what is about to take place, when suddenly an urge to run back towards the restaurant overcomes me.

"Pick me up at La Parrilla," I command the driver.

By now the man has exited the restaurant and is dragging the hysterical Silvia behind him. She is kicking and fighting and clawing at the man with all her might; but there is nothing she can do to weaken her husband's grip on her. "Son of a bitch!" she screams. "Put me down!"

"Shut up!" the man yells back, groping her face with his hand to try and cover her mouth.

What transpires next I am hard pressed to describe. I see Silvia stiffen in her husband's grip; she shuts her eyes tightly and lets go a cry so visceral in its intensity that I am physically stunned. Never have I heard such an outburst of anguish, though I once heard descriptions of such hellish screams originating from the underground torture cells of the federal police. Abruptly, I stop in the middle of the road and listen in awe as her powerful lungs continue to expel these harrowing sounds. I see her breath now in a ray of light, visible to the world, the voice of Silvia, echoing off the snow-covered mountains with an unnatural force. By the doorway of the restaurant I see the old man with the cane watching the struggle in the street as it unfolds. Slowly, mechanically, he moves his arm across his chest in the sign of the cross and mumbles to himself a precautionary prayer. Behind him the proprietress looks quietly over his shoulder, awash in the waxy yellow light that pours out onto the street.

The man opens the door and pushes his wife into the car.

It is a futile gesture, but I chase after the car as it slides through the snow, cursing the brutality of Silvia's kidnapping. The car disappears behind a bend, and the sputtering of its engine can no longer be heard. In a daze, I walk back to the bus and slump into a seat next to Alvarez, who is staring out the window, immersed in some erudite reverie. He turns, pats me sympathetically on the shoulder. As he speaks to me in that articulate, logical way of his, in the manner of one who is never to be doubted — so much in authority, so deserving of the layman's confidence and belief — I suddenly realize that it is Alvarez who produces the more bewitching of human intonations, that his is in fact a damnable voice, a voice of conviction and certainty promulgated for his own egotistical pleasures, exaggerated for the sake of influence and distortion.

"A philosopher once wrote," he says with an air of self-importance, "that beauty and ugliness are twigs of the same branch."

"You produced a very clever hoax in there, Sr. Alvarez," I reply, discomfited by the nostrum of this fraud. "The only siren we heard tonight is sitting right here beside me, though it was the devil's tune and not God's that was trumpeted."

Alvarez smiles, then pulls out his pipe and loads it with tobacco. He strikes a match on the back of the seat in front of him, draws on his pipe, and directs a stream of sweet smelling tobacco out the window. "One day," he says, as if talking to himself, "I will return to this valley — one day before I grow too old and lose all my hearing — so that I may listen once again to the magnificent voice of that woman. She is remarkable, and I enjoyed her reading immensely."

The gearshift grinds and locks into place. Our bus heaves forward onto the snowy mountain road with sharp, mechanical creaks, and as we speed towards the first bend I watch the snowflakes whirl fitfully outside my window. In the seat pocket in front of me rests the book that Silvia read from — a collection of poems written by a Spaniard named Carlos Almeria. Tucked into the book is the ten peso note that she either neglected to pocket or refused to accept, perhaps considering my gesture an affront to her dignity: it bookmarks the poem called "Indelible" that she so eloquently read to us tonight — verse intoned, some would now believe, with echoes of immortal whispers — a poem that I hereby resolve to commit, indelibly as it were, to memory.

The Portenian

One day, in the winter of 1985, I went exploring an old area of downtown Buenos Aires known as San Telmo. It was Sunday, the day the vendors set up their stalls along the walkways in the plaza, laying out old paintings, Victrolla phonographs, brass trumpets, sextants, eighteenth century cutlery, anything old and useless but endearing enough to fetch a few *australes*. It was cold and cloudy. The sky broke out in low rumbles now and then, prompting worried looks from the vendors. One man standing with folded arms by an antique clock saw me walking by and, in the deft manner of all hawkers, drew my attention to his collection of nineteenth century pocket watches, one of which struck my fancy.

"*Un tesoro,*" he proclaimed, and handed me the silver Longines watch. It was smooth, had that worn, polished look of an old silver coin that had been passed from pocket to pocket for the greater part of a century. I opened it, and watched in fascination the tiny gears grind away the time. Made in 1876, it was indeed a fine piece.

"I can give you fifty *australes*."

The vendor laughed. His wrinkled face and smooth, greased back hair gave him an antique look himself, as though he belonged to the epoch of his wares. "That watch," he said, "belonged to the governor of the province of Buenos Aires. It has historical value beyond the value of the watch itself."

"Is that so?" I frowned at the vendor. "All right," I said. "Sixty *australes*."

"No," he said, pretending offense, "surely you recognize the fine condition of the governor's watch. The fact that it still works is a marvel in itself."

I suddenly grew weary of the negotiations. I threw up my hands and walked away.

Tired, I sat on a bench under a massive *ombú* tree whose thick, octopus branches spread out horizontally for several meters. An elderly man was sitting on the other end of the bench as if someone had left him there. His sad, walrus eyes were barely open, and his flat, sagging face and small head seemed set in stone. He turned very slowly and peered at me for several moments, his eyes squinting in an effort to focus, to conjure an image of who it was that had taken a seat beside him.

"Looks like it may rain today," I said.

The elderly man leaned back to look at the sky, but the branches of the *ombú* in fact covered such a view.

"It feels like rain," he said. "Yes, I can feel it."

Not five seconds had passed when suddenly it came after us, dripping as if through gutter spouts between the branches of the tree.

The old man had an umbrella. He opened it, and said: "You are welcome to share this umbrella with me. As you can see, it's quite large."

I slid over beneath his umbrella and thanked him.

"There's a café on the corner," I said.

"Yes," the old man countered. "I am familiar with it."

"Why don't we take shelter there? I'll buy you a cup of coffee."

"Very well."

I took my guest by the arm and led him across the cobblestone street to a spot beneath the gold awning of Greco's Café. I folded the umbrella and handed it to the waiter at the door, who bowed to the old man and bade him good day and welcome, as though he had served him often. The café was dark, continental, its stained mahogany paneling contrasting strongly against the stiff white tablecloths and crystal chandeliers. Several waiters in black bow ties and vests stood by at attention.

We were seated. Our waiter, a tall, fair-skinned man with Italian features handed us a menu.

"You know," I said. "I haven't eaten anything today. Would you join me for some lunch?"

The old man smiled. "Of course."

My guest ordered fish. I ordered the *bife de lomo*. We also ordered a bottle of red wine.

"I never asked your name," I said.

"Why don't we pretend," he said wryly, "that we are men without names. Strangers only. Men who met in the rain and decided to have lunch together."

The audacity of his comment made me a laugh.

"All right," I said. "Suppose we keep our occupations secret as well. Instead of, say, a cello player meeting a doctor in the rain one Sunday afternoon, we'll say simply that two men met in the rain and decided to have lunch together."

The old gentlemen nodded. "Suppose we keep our personal histories in check as well. So that, instead of Ramón the cello player from Córdoba meeting Enrique the doctor from Tucumán, we are simply an old man and a younger man, whom we know very little about. We do not know, for instance, from what country this young man's people immigrated; whether he is married, has children, owns his own home or rents an apartment; whether he drives a BMW or a Ford, wears tailor-made suits or buys them directly off the rack. Maybe he was taunted and beaten by bullies as a child, or was dishonorably discharged from the army for stealing. Possibly he's had an illicit affair with his secretary, or is wanted by the police for the commission of a heinous crime, such as murder. None of it matters. None of it concerns us. And so, you see, suddenly we are forced to talk about issues other than ourselves."

I sipped some of the fine Mendozan cabernet, and quietly considered the possibility that he had spent some time in prison. This might account for his reluctance to speak about the past; but, as I saw none of the roughness that such experience might etch into the demeanor and speech of the convict, I concluded that he was simply following a whimsical train of thought for his own amusement.

"Well," I said. "It's really none of my business."

"Besides—," he said, trailing off. His head was titled to one side, quietly lost in thought.

"Yes?"

"I'm just wondering … about this opportunity that we seem to have."

"I'm not sure that I follow," I said.

"Yes. We could have a little fun with this."

"I'm afraid you've lost me."

He laughed at my confusion. "Think about it," he said. "Unlike most strangers who meet for the first time, we have, in exercising our wits, chosen to deny ourselves an identity. The implications are staggering, perhaps even profound."

"How do you mean?"

"I mean that we are now, in a sense, liberated, disconnected from our own impish personal concerns. The uniqueness of the situation allows us now to investigate each others insights and observations without reference to our past."

"But for what purpose?"

"I don't know. For the hell of it I suppose. In any event, if we are to conduct this little experiment, you must agree to leave out your own identity and personal experience."

I hastened to consider what he was alluding to. "I wonder if that is really possible — whether one can separate so easily what one knows from who one is. Surely the sum of a person's experience influences his view of the world."

"No. Not entirely."

He said this with such certainty that I realized refuting this assertion would be a waste of breath, which annoyed me; so I said nothing.

"As a corollary to this," he said, "wouldn't it be something to make a clean break of one's more cumbersome influences?"

My annoyance now grew into a kind of intellectual cowardice: I feared that I was about to be lured into a kind of Socratic dialogue: Socrates, after all, was a man capable of rationalizing anything, of making reasonable people look foolish in order to lend credence to his own views.

"I don't know," I said. "I like knowing where I come from."

A basket of French bread was brought to us. I tore into a piece, realizing that I was famished.

"You know," I said. "I used to roam these streets as a boy, hungry to the point of stealing bread, like this, from the grocers, who were kind enough to pretend not to notice. Those experiences made me what I am, made me feel the way I do. I can't deny that."

The old man frowned. "I'm not concerned with your personal regrets about the cruelty of life. Of course that makes you feel the way you do. I am blind. Imagine the injustice of blindness, and wonder if it ever makes me angry."

"Well then. Why not take pride in the influences which made us who we are?"

"No reason. All I am saying is that maybe we can be more than just that, more than just the cumulative sum of our parochial influences."

"Be more specific," I said.

"I mean, for example, to wake up one day and find yourself alone in a strange city with amnesia. You wander about the streets for days, looking for clues to your past identity, until finally one day you give up altogether, and forge ahead into a new one."

I looked into my companion's eyes, watching for signs that he really could see.

"You seem to enjoy being cryptic," I said.

"I will tell you something," the old gentleman said, gazing at me with those dead eyes of his. "I am old now, eighty-six in fact, and will probably die one day very soon. What I want to suggest to you, in my own cryptic way, is that I have lived and died many times now in the span of my eighty-six years."

"Metaphorically, of course."

"Of course," he said.

"I must admit that I don't see much point to all this. Aren't we in fact getting to know one another, in spite of the fact that so far we haven't said much of anything about who we are?"

"Maybe we know each other better now than we might have by doing nothing but talking about ourselves."

"But what if I were a genius in, say, astronomy. Without knowing that I was an astronomer, how would you know to ask me about the nature of comets and meteors?"

"I wouldn't. But it's likely that if I wanted to find out about comets and meteors, I would find out who to speak to about them."

"Still. You would have lost an opportunity for insight, as you call it. You would never have known that you could have accessed a vast amount of knowledge about the stars."

"Right now," my blind guest said, "you could be an expert in any field, not just astronomy. Without knowing exactly what your field of study is, I am free to imagine that you hold vast amounts of knowledge about a variety of different fields. Isn't that far more interesting? To know that I could be an expert on anything, instead of only one or two things which I openly declare?"

"I don't know," I said, "breaking with one's influences is fine if those influences happen to make a nightmare of your life. I know many people who fall into that category."

"No. That's not the point. I told you. I'm not interested in parting with the past because it happens to be ugly. That's another matter entirely. I'm talking about not letting these influences dictate who you are, who you wish to become. Perhaps," the old man said, "I can explain it another way. I'm constantly being told that all Argentine writers, for example, must write about Argentine themes, use florid local colors to describe scenery, write about tangos and gauchos and characters that say "*che*" and drink *mate*. Why is that? Why can't an Argentine writer write about universal themes, like space and time, beauty or despair, without having to constantly pay homage to national idiosyncrasies?"

I stared at the old man in a kind of shock. I understood him perfectly now. Everything he had alluded to. All this meandering about identity. All these mental contortions.

I sat back in my chair and gazed for a moment at the chandelier above our table. The old gentlemen shifted nervously in his seat and jut forth his long, flat face, knowing, sensing that something had changed. "You just asked that we not give ourselves away," I said.

This statement took the old man by surprise. He seemed to shudder, to quiver slightly in what I took to be a paroxysm of disquietude.

"Oh," he said, his voice tinged with a kind of melancholy resignation. "You read fiction, do you?"

"Yes. Enough to know that there is only one well known writer in Argentina who feels that way, in spite of the fact that he has written stories about gauchos. He is old now, and blind — like you."

The waiter brought out our food. We took up our forks and knives and began slicing our entrees.

Jorge Luis Borges spoke little for the remainder of the meal; our conversation had, inexplicably, come to an abrupt end, in spite of the efforts I made to keep it alive. I regretted that our pact had been broken. I regretted, in spite of my disagreement with his logic regarding the nature of our conversation, that were we no longer anonymous men who had met one afternoon in the rain and decided to have lunch together, no longer strangers afforded an unusual opportunity to investigate each other's insights and observations. Having meandered through his maze of stories as a boy, having lost myself in his Garden of Forking Paths and Circular Ruins, I knew only too well the sublime ruminations of this erudite old man; yet I saw none of that now. I did not see Borges in that moment as the profound and visionary writer that the world knew him to be. Instead, I saw a man with an affliction of self-consciousness that, I suppose, only the well known can fully comprehend.

At one point I said: "You know. In a sense I am sorry that I've found you out, Señor Borges. In another, I am glad, because now our conversation means something more than just a young man and an old man speaking in a vacuum, airing existential ideas and theories without attaching any personal history to them. I have read your works; and I consider our meeting in this way a great pleasure and an honor."

"That may be," he replied. "You may know me better now, or think you do, but not because I talked about myself as a writer or discussed why writing about certain themes is important to me. Our conversation may now have a certain context for you, but it was never simply words in a vacuum."

Our meal was only half finished when Borges suddenly stood up from the table. "My driver will pick me up soon," he said. "Don't bother showing me out. Good day. And thank you."

I stood up and shook his hand.

"Señor Borges," I said. "You once wrote a piece called *Borges and I* in which you suggested that there were two of you — the one who writes stories — and the other Borges, the one formed as a result of the literature that Borges writes. This other Borges, the fictional one, is described walking the streets of Buenos Aires, living his own life, having his own tastes, but unsure of his own reality. You concluded the piece by stating that you were unsure of which Borges had written it."

The old man was smiling at me now, almost mockingly; and in a moment that can only be described as terrible, I realized, surmised, deduced *that I had been speaking to the fictional Borges all along.* It was absurd, of course; even so, this notion overwhelmed my brain with its curiously aesthetical symmetry. A part of me actually believed that I had in fact just dined with a figment conjured from the pen of a famous writer, a Portenian phantom come to life, wandering the streets and parks of the capital, riding, perhaps, in a subway train or standing in a crowded bus, imbued by his maker with a formidable intellect but recognizing himself more in the nameless, blurred faces that he encounters — in the vendors of antiquities in the plaza of San Telmo or in the voice of a stranger that he lunches with — than in the labyrinthine body of literature which justifies him and gives him life.

"So. Which is it? Which Borges am I addressing?" I demanded to know.

"I wish I knew," he said, reaching for his umbrella.

"Tell me," I said, as he ambled toward the door. "Is it possible that it was not your identity that we stumbled over in our little experiment to communicate anonymously, but instead the lack of it?"

"It is possible," he replied, "that my identity has nothing to do with gathering an understanding of the world. Good afternoon."

* * *

I wandered back to the plaza. The rain was gone, having now frozen into small, white pellets of hail, which fell sporadically from the sky, pelting the cobblestone streets like glass beads. The *ombú* tree dripped water like tears from its immense canopy, and as I stood there in the cold with folded arms, shivering and yearning for the pleasure of a cigarette, all the melancholy, all the lamentation and nostalgia inherent in the artesian soul of the Argentine came rushing into my thoughts, overwhelming me with a bittersweet mixture of contentment and regret.

The vendor was still there, huddled beneath a tarpaulin, a smile on his stubbly face. I laughed at the site of him, and offered him one hundred australes for the Longines watch.

"Would you believe," I said to the vendor, "that I just had lunch with Jorge Luis Borges?"

The vendor thumbed rapidly through the ten austral notes. "You don't say," he said. "And who might that be?"

A Chance Meeting At Luigi's Café

I met Sergio Palacios in 1980, in that dreadful epoch of fear and violence now known as the "Dirty War". We met by way of a mutual friend — Leonardo Garibaldi — who, like Palacios, did research in neuroscience at the University of Buenos Aires. Leonardo, a rotund, dark-haired man with luminous blue eyes, was a sociable type. He entertained small gatherings at his flat in Palermo where, amidst the strumming of a Spanish guitar, a cabal of academics surveyed the issues of the day, their fiery rhetoric punctuated with poignant, eloquent flashes of insight. They laughed frequently and with abandon, drank heavily, argued heatedly, and reveled in the chaotic exchange of ideas, though Leonardo admitted that he had become disappointed with its direction into "nihilism and irrelevance". Like many I'd had the pleasure of knowing during my business trips to Buenos Aires, Leonardo was curious about the latest happenings in the States; and as he often invited me to contribute a "foreign point of view" to their social discussions (albeit painfully, in my stilted, laconic Spanish) he took it upon himself to educate me, in a rather paternal way, on the way of life — the *forma de ser* — of the Argentine *porteño*.

One day in April, as we were making our way down Juramento in search of our favorite café — the low sky bearing down on us with a leaden grayness and the dry leaves rustling down the cobbled streets with soft, scratching sounds — I met, for the first time, Sergio Palacios. He gave me an effusive shake of the hand and poured forth an envious abundance of the Argentine charm. It was impossible not to like him. His self-deprecating humor, his florid, concise style of articulation, were striking, and I later remarked to Garibaldi that Palacios had impressed me as a pleasantly modest type for someone of his stature.

"Yes. There is not a pretentious bone in his body," Garibaldi remarked after we had said our *chaus* to Sergio. He looked askance at me as we walked across the park, his large jaw flexing in anticipation of his next thought. "But don't be fooled, Richard. The man you just met is one of the most brilliant men in Argentina. His mind is capable of grasping complexities you and I could never comprehend; but he's not always taken seriously, and is in fact often dismissed for his utopian sensibilities." Garibaldi went on to make various other comments about Sergio: how he was often seen wandering about the damp capitol streets of Buenos Aires with his shoulders hunched; how his greenish-stained teeth betrayed an over-indulgence in *mate* tea, which he drank almost religiously. "I personally don't drink *mate*," Leonardo said. "But Sergio is a fanatic — not so much of the tea itself but of the etiquette and social ceremony involved in the serving and drinking of *mate*. I've heard rumors that Sergio takes advantage of this custom to encourage censured political discussion in his apartment in Belgrano. But the people who say these things either dislike him or misunderstand him."

One night Garibaldi and I met at Luigi's Café on Santa Fe Avenue, not far from Sergio's place. We were each finishing the last bites of an empanada when Garibaldi suddenly sputtered through a mouthful of food that he saw Palacios coming out of the cinema across the street. Garibaldi and I hastened out the door and called him over to join us. Palacios, surprised, waved and headed our way.

Two men wearing black jackets followed Palacios out of the theater. They stopped behind him as we hailed Sergio, and, thrusting their hands in their pockets, quietly studied us from the curb. As they spoke to one another they threw short glances our way. They took out packets of cigarettes. One of them nodded in our direction as he lit his companion's *pucho*, and the two of them strained to look at Garibaldi and I through the throng of honking cars and trucks. The lead man, a tall, straw-haired man with a calm, resolved manner, wandered over to a kiosk and paid for a Coke. He sat on a bus bench and crossed his legs. The other man took out a comb and ran it through his hair, then put away his comb and began nervously flicking the ash from his cigarette as he looked in our direction.

Sergio was panting for breath by the time he reached us. He greeted Leonardo with an *abrazo* — the customary embrace of the Argentine — after which he grabbed Leonardo by the back of the neck and stapled a kiss onto his cheek. The thought of him kissing me as well — I could already smell the stench of the Gitanes cigarettes on his breath — prompted me to back off, but before I could get clear away Palacios had grabbed me by the shoulders and was hugging me as if I were the brother he never had.

"Hello! How are you?" he said in English.

My friend Leonardo gave a snort of dissatisfaction. "It's not unusual for Argentine men to kiss each other," he assured me. "It's a gesture of friendship, nothing else." I was of course embarrassed by the offense I'd given, but only made matters worse by telling him that they could kiss each other all they liked, for all I cared. When I finished this awkward apology, Garibaldi, whom I suspected of being a perfect bully as a child, laughed at me in a daring fashion, as if he were just begging me to question the integrity of his masculinity.

Our waiter was scowling at us from a distance, so we sat down at our table and ordered "water with gas".

"So. You are from the United States," Sergio said, this time in Spanish. He was eyeing me with great curiosity.

"Yes. He's working for a big oil company downtown," Garibaldi said. "His assignment, as I understand it, is to screw the gullible Latinos out of their natural resources." He gave Sergio an emphatic wink.

"Well, well," Palacios said, shaking his finger at me. "Up to your old Yankee tricks, are you?"

Our waiter approached. "You want something else?"

Leonardo lit a cigarette and held up his thumb and forefinger in a gesture that the waiter immediately recognized as *cortado*, or coffee cut with cream. "And bring one for my American friend here, who is an honored guest in our country, and who sometimes goes by the name of Cholo."

Palacios laughed. "Leonardo was a gangster in a previous life," he told me.

Garibaldi frowned and began to work his jaw, flexing it repeatedly while his eyes roamed about the room. He leaned across the table toward Sergio, and whispered: "*Che*. What have you been up to, Sergio? Eh? Who are those two thugs across the street?"

"What are you talking about? What thugs?"

"Two guys were watching you as you left the theater," I said.

"*Ojo*," observed Garibaldi, pulling on his lower eyelid with his forefinger in the Argentine gesture meaning *watch out*. "The army has spies all over the university, watching and snooping around like rats. The other day I got a visit from one of these son of a bitches. He took my manuscript, and I haven't gotten it back yet."

"Why would they take your manuscript?" I asked.

"Because," Garibaldi replied, smirking, "they're frightened of people who exhibit any kind of brains."

Such comments, I found, were not unusual at the time, especially from the cloistered underground of the intelligentsia. I was aware that the military was attempting to stamp out the last remnants of the guerrilla movement led by the Montoneros and Trotskyites, which had terrorized and bombed its way into the very heart of the capitol. One read about such things in the paper: bomb blasts, shootings, kidnappings, demands, army counterattacks and offensives; and I quickly learned that, in light of the gruesome upheaval that had become for the Argentine an unbearable routine, a general agreement had been reached — a rather ignoble social contract, as it turned out — that the army should be empowered to put an end to the terrorist threat, even if it meant overriding the rule of law and the suspension of certain civil liberties. History now shows that the military abused this mandate, that they kept the public in the dark concerning the details of their mission to rid the country of anarchists and guerrillas, resulting in the prevailing uneasiness, the collective confusion brought on by "The Process". I once brought up the subject of *Los Desaparecidos* (The Disappeared) during a social engagement, and was told, in no uncertain terms, that this was something that wasn't talked about.

"I try," Palacios said. "But it's like you say. Anyone with half a brain is considered a terrorist. In fact I recently had a visit of my own from one of these military spies. He came into my office about two weeks ago, demanding full access to my files. I of course refused, and the next day I found my office ransacked, my papers gone. When I returned home I found my apartment had also been ransacked. They had found my notes on artificial cognition, and have been following me ever since."

"What possible interest could the army have in your research?" I asked.

"They could reap political benefits from it."

"From what? Artificial cognition?"

"Yes."

"I wasn't aware you were working on artificial intelligence, Sergio." Garibaldi said this with obvious surprise.

"No, no. This has nothing to do with computers."

"Well then, what?"

Palacios seemed unwillingly to go on. He looked warily at Leonardo, as if he feared him, then launched into a fantastic story of how it would soon be possible to design drugs to influence our thought patterns and behaviors; in effect, to chemically program ideologies, turning the leftist into the conservative, the fundamentalist into the humanist, the misanthrope into the philanthropist, and vice versa. "Neuroscience will one day free us," he said, as if doubting such a notion would be idiotic. "It will give us choices we never had before, liberating us from the tyranny of our own genetic faults. We can live with our flaws if we choose to — our evolutionary baggage of violence and aggression and other such instinctive appetites. But we will also have the choice of rejecting these biological imperfections."

"*Mierda*," Garibaldi replied in disbelief. He let out a moan, and placed the tips of his fingers against his forehead, which he gently rubbed as he stared into his cup of coffee. He was hugely embarrassed, and was no doubt wondering what I was thinking of his visionary friend and his exotic ideas. I recalled Garibaldi's prior characterization of Sergio being both exalted and dismissed by his peers, and smiled at the irony of this understatement.

"So. Now the military has this information," I said.

"Yes," Sergio admitted. "But I doubt they could establish a proof of concept."

"They might if they coerced you," I said, thinking aloud.

This *faux pas* (or *papelón* in the Argentine vernacular) provoked an outraged look from Leonardo, whose displeasure was accentuated by his habitual jaw grinding. "We are very well aware of that possibility," he said, regaining some composure. "As you well know we live under military rule here; what you may not know, because it is never reported in the newspapers, is that we're in the throes of an urban war that's killing thousands of innocents. People disappear here every day. I know. Some of my best friends have been snatched from their homes by the military and never heard from again."

The restaurant had grown quiet. Many of the diners were staring at us with stern, reproaching faces. Disconcerted by these glares, I looked out the window and saw the two shadows that had followed Palacios out of the cinema still sitting across the street on the bench. The straw-haired man was looking directly at me now. He seemed to smile at me through the clouds of exhaust fumes.

"*Mierda*," Leonardo said again. My thoughts were somewhere along those lines, except that I was beginning to feel more inclined to consider the potential consequence of Sergio's speculations, ridiculous though they were. In retrospect, I considered him brave, in his own illegitimate way, for reaching out to the unknown, for striving to embrace the sublime chemicals and spiritual currents that formed the foundation of his own highly intelligent electro-chemical imagination.

I didn't see much of either Leonardo or Sergio after our last meeting: we avoided each other with tactful excuses. Better, I thought, that we should be left alone to flinch at our recent encounter with Sergio's constructively managed world, where the essential substance of humanity, with its antipodes of beauty and ugliness, purity and corruption, is reduced to a mere subset of molecular configurations. The fact that Garibaldi and I had found it necessary to rebut these flights of imagination on moral and scientific grounds made it even more painful to remember. Still, in spite of all this, my opinion of Sergio Palacios was ameliorated with the passing of time. I realized that in a world replete with dullness and mediocrity he stood out amongst the crowd, possessing a rare quality which, in contrast to the diffused comfort we find in ignorance, announces itself in the most cogent and unsettling of forms. His imagination was a labyrinth of complexity, and I began to see that it commanded much more from us than a grudging, judgmental, inadequate respect for his intellectual versatility. It required, I think, a certain homage, if not outright veneration, by those of us knew who him and who could laugh at him openly while at the same moment admiring the profoundness and penetration of his vision.

As for Garibaldi, my trips to Palermo soon came to an end. Sadly, I no longer felt welcome to profit from his instruction on the ways of the *porteño*.

* * *

I left Buenos Aires soon after and did not return for another six years, long after the military had failed in its vain-glorious attempt to divert attention away from their economic and social failures by way of a heroic Falkland Islands invasion. The old conquistadors, nostalgic to the end, hung up their berets. Meanwhile the graduates of the Che Guevara School — the Montoneros and the Trotskyites — lost out to the public's indifference to their utopian demands, and were now licking their wounds underground, in Cuba, or in El Salvador. It was a new epoch, a promising new period. A new president was elected — a grandfatherly type who people trusted not to invade distant lands, one who would promise to fix the national debt and would graciously welcome the Yankee gringos and their bagsful of investment dollars.

It was the last night of my visit. I walked from our office on Florida Street through St. Martin Plaza and on to the Retiro train station. There I bought a ticket on the El Tigre train with a stop at the suburb of Martinez, where I would have dinner and stay the night with a colleague and his family before being taken to Ezeiza airport the next morning by taxi.

The train was packed as usual. People shuffled in, searching for seats, their red eyes hungry for relief. They rummaged their pockets for tickets, which they held out to be snipped by the conductor who slowly made his way down the aisle. In a few minutes the electric train lurched forward, sloshing the standing passengers to the backs of their heels or into the person next to them. A man with an ice cream cooler strapped to his stomach opened the car and began singing: *"Helado-o-o-s. Bien fríos! Helado-o-o-s."* He was followed by the same blind harmonica player who had frequented the station and its trains some six years earlier. He blew one of the happy tunes I remembered he used to play, and then wandered down the aisle with a canvas bag to collect a few australes. I saw one woman place a wad of old pesos into the sack. She looked over at me, annoyed that I had seen her place worthless, outdated currency into the poor blind man's donation bag. As she got up to disembark at the Olivos station I suddenly caught a glimpse of Garibaldi's profile at the back of the car. He stood waiting for the doors to swish open, a satchel in one hand and an umbrella in the other. He looked much older than I knew his years to be; his hair was now completely gray and his face was lined and his chin was beginning to sag. He glanced furtively in my direction, and I knew immediately that he had seen me, knew I was in the same car, and was hoping to escape unnoticed.

The doors slid open with a sudden hiss. Leonardo Garibaldi disembarked.

"Leonardo!" I cried. "Leonardo Garibaldi!"

I ran towards him, but as the mass of bodies funneling out the door prevented me from approaching him, I ran to an open window and hailed him again as he walked along the platform with downcast eyes.

"Leonardo! It's me — Richard Cook!"

Garibaldi kept walking. I followed him with my eyes. Then he stopped, turned slowly around, and stood looking at me with glowering impatience. His teeth were grinding furiously, and there was a wild, explosive look of rage in his bloodshot eyes.

"What happened to Sergio?" I yelled.

The train had already lurched forward and Garibaldi was by now far away, just barely within earshot. He yelled something about a man on the train — I couldn't make out exactly what he was referring to — but one word came across with a guttural clarity:

"*Disappeared.*"

Beside me came a scuffing of feet, and the sound of an impatient voice. "Tickets," it said. I looked up, and saw the conductor, whose striking features seemed oddly familiar, standing before me. As I searched my coat the conductor waived his puncher before me like a crab claw, clicking this pincer with a maddening rapidity. He leered at me as I handed him my passage, and I knew in an instant that I had seen him somewhere before, years ago, though I wasn't yet sure of the time or the place. A sense of foreboding overwhelmed me. He seemed to sense this. He was watching me carefully, when he said, abruptly: "Your friend died five years ago, Mr. Cook." A little smile crossed his face at the effect of this revelation, because I realized that this conductor, whose straw-colored hair fell unevenly beneath his cap, was the man that Garibaldi had fled the train in fear of.

The Lagerstätten

I.

One day in January — January 12th to be exact — we found ourselves standing on a pass between two snow-capped peaks at 4,700 meters altitude, gasping for breath and struggling against the pounding headaches produced by the lack of oxygen. My brother Roberto reminded me that it was my turn to fill the canteens, so I started down the rocky slope, heading straight for the small streams that branched off the meandering glacier of cracked blue ice in the valley below us. I descended into a narrow swath of shadow, switch-backing my way toward the glacier's edge; and there, on that barren, Cordilleran slope, I found the layer of rock that we later christened the Cavazos Formation. Scanning the terrain, I thought my mind was playing tricks on me. The altitude perhaps — I knew that climbers in the Andes occasionally suffered delusions induced by hypoxia. But the strange forms I saw in the rocks were solid and immovable. All around me, stamped into the millions of rock shards sloughed off the outcrops by the extremes of heat and cold, lay frozen impressions of Cretaceous-aged fauna, some of them displaying attributes of both plant and animal, as if Nature, through that sudden and sporadic change process known by the evolutionary biologists as Punctuated Equilibrium, had given birth to a hybrid of the taxonomic kingdoms. I picked up a flat piece of shale that hosted an ammonite whose spiral shape had evolved from a tight coil into that of a perfect figure nine, and held it up in the air with both hands. "Get down here," I yelled to Roberto and his student Elena. "Both of you. Come take a look at this."

Within the span of an hour we found hundreds of aquatic animal species scattered amongst the incline, embedded in the wine-colored shale — a graveyard that no paleontological textbook or monograph had ever described

— replete with evolutionary dead-ends whose lineages had been doomed to a cruel obscurity. As we scoured the slope, picking over the talus for more fossils, we paused to listen to each other's shouted descriptions of an undiscovered species or, in the rare case, the potential for a new branch in the tree of life. I remember the smiles on our faces as we scurried along the slope, finding fossil after fossil — none of them familiar — outlines of one hundred and forty million-year-old animals so perfectly preserved you could see their cilia, their tiny octopus-like tentacles, their spiny teeth — even the outlines of their feathery, soft-bodied forms. We also found fossil casts of enormous shark teeth, dark gray in color, with sharp, serrated ridges along the edges. They were monstrous things, the size of a large man's hand, remnants of a cavernous jaw.

The sun soon dipped below the pass, enveloping the windy cirque valley in cold shadows, in alpine harshness. We made camp on a level spot by the glacier. After feeding the horses, Elena made a frugal dinner of dried beef and hot soup, which we ate while discussing the various samples that we had collected. Roberto heated a pot of glacial ice to make the *mate* tea. He poured a gourdful, added a spoonful of sugar, and passed it to Elena, who sucked the hot green broth from the metal straw and warmed her hands on the gourd before passing it to me. We sat in a circle around the small cook-stove, cleaning and studying the fossils and remarking on the unusual aspects of their morphology. Elena kept laughing and grinning and talking excitedly. She was an attractive woman, in spite of the dirt that had accumulated on her over the last several weeks, regardless of her bruises and scratches and disheveled, wavy hair.

Roberto rubbed his hands over the stove. "There's a word for finds like this," he said. "They call them *Lagerstätten*. They are so rare that only a handful have ever been found: one formation in British Columbia called the Burgess Shale. Another few in the United States. One in

Germany called the *Solnhofen*, where they found the first bird, *Archaeopteryx*."

"I don't recall that term," I replied. "But I recognize the names of those formations."

"*Lagerstätten* means 'lode places' in German. Think of them as paleontological Mother Lodes — a rich and diverse class of fossil beds with spectacular preservation. Some of our most invaluable insights into natural history have come from these rocks."

"I've read that some of the fossils that come out of those beds are worth tens of thousands of dollars," Elena reflected. "Are you saying we've found something comparable?"

"Yes. That's exactly what I'm saying."

Each of us quietly pondered the implications of this and considered the task ahead of us; namely, we had to carry the fossils out, safely, and maintain strict confidence of the location of our discovery long enough for us to return and extract from the area the most precious and valuable specimens we could find.

We had wandered into this area by accident, and were still unsure of our exact location. Our handheld GPS had fallen onto some rocks only two days into our expedition and, as we could never get it to function again, we navigated solely by means of compass and map, knowing that the available maps of the region were considered untrustworthy. We fretted over the possibility that we might never successfully backtrack to this remote region that, for all we knew, had never been previously explored by geologists.

Elena took out one of the map quadrants we had come to rely on and found an outline of a glacier in a narrow valley. After studying the map a few moments, she declared: "We came down this pass here — but the border doesn't follow the ridgeline as one might expect. Instead it zigzags on either side of it in several places, dipping into this valley and showing most of this glacier on the Argentine side of the line."

Roberto took the map, studied it, and ultimately agreed with her assessment. The border between Argentina and Chile snaked widely on both sides of the ridge and was marked with a dotted line, indicated in the map legend as a contested boundary. "I don't trust this map," he remarked, scanning the peaks with a frown, "but it does seem likely that we're in disputed territory here."

Later that evening we exchanged ideas on the reasons for the unusual quality of the fossil preservation. "If your company hadn't snubbed us when it came time to fund this work," Roberto said, "you'd have been considered an equal partner. As it is, the university will expect Elena and I to do the paperwork."

It was a rather insipid attack, and had less to do with the whims of an older brother than with his underlying need to assert his dominance and authority over the direction of our investigation. He felt threatened by my contributions — why I don't know. To make matters worse, I overheard Roberto later that night as he slipped out of our tent and into Elena's, ostensibly to discuss a technical issue. I lay awake for hours that night, as did they, and listened to them laugh with the untethered abandon that accompanies the realization of good fortune. They were giddy with excitement, acting like children who spitefully ignore their friends. Well. It didn't matter that my company had refused to fund this expedition. Why should it? After all, its interest lay in minerals, not fossils.

II.

We spent the next five days on the slopes of the glacial valley. Roberto and Elena made detailed descriptions of the fossils, took hundreds of photographs, plotted spatial distributions, and made preliminary taxonomic categorizations. I mapped the lateral extent of the source formation and began a detailed biostratigraphic zoning of the rock column. But I soon grew bored with this tedious work, and wandered off by myself into an adjoining valley where I found an outcrop streaked with small veins of what appeared to be silver. I took several samples for lab analysis, and when I returned to camp Roberto and Elena asked me if I had found any fossils in the adjoining valley. I told them no, that there was nothing there that would interest them.

One late afternoon, as we sat huddled around our cook stove drinking *mate*, we saw a small figure standing on the horizon on a crag of rock, looking down into the valley.

"Who do you suppose that is?" Roberto asked.

The tiny figure continued to watch us.

Elena fetched the binoculars and focused on the mysterious speck. "It's a gendarme," she said. "A border guard."

"How do you know that? You can't possibly tell that from here, even with binoculars."

"Yes," she said. "I recognize the color of his uniform."

"Is it one of ours?"

"No. He's Chilean. He's heading this way."

"Cover the samples," Roberto said.

"No. That's not a good idea," Elena warned. "Better not make any hasty movements. He's been watching us with binoculars too. He'd immediately become suspicious if we started covering up things. Just sit still."

Twenty minutes later a man dressed in fatigues, carrying a heavy pack and a semi-automatic rifle, strode up into camp. He was young, no more than twenty-five. He smiled and waved at us as he approached, as if to allay the suspicion that he saw frozen on our dirty, savage-looking faces.

"*Buenas tardes,*" he said, smiling. He took off his cap and wiped his brow. He looked tired.

"*Buenas tardes*," Roberto replied, nodding and standing up. He introduced us by name and explained that we were researchers on a geological expedition from the University of Buenos Aires.

The young man frowned slightly when he heard this. "What kind of geological expedition? he asked.

"We're looking for fossils," Elena said.

The young man slid off his pack and sat down on a rock. He kept his semi-automatic cradled snugly in his arms, but gave every appearance of congeniality. "You aren't doing any mineral exploration, are you?" he asked in a serious tone.

"No, no," I said. "There aren't any minerals in these rocks."

Elena offered the gendarme a gourd of *mate*, which he accepted graciously. He took the gourd with two hands and smiled, revealing a gold front tooth. "Do you have permission to be here?" he asked.

"How do you mean?" Roberto returned. "We're on Argentine soil."

The young man frowned again. "No," he said. "I'm afraid not. This entire valley resides in Chile."

"Our maps say differently," Roberto said, his voice registering an obvious irritation and impatience.

The young man tactfully changed the subject. "This is good *mate*," he said, smiling. "It's been days since I've had one. Would you have any food that you could spare? I'm heading back to San Jorge tomorrow and am running a little low."

"Yes," Elena said. "I'll get you some. How much do you need?"

"Oh, no more than three day's worth. If you could spare me that much, I'd be very grateful." The gendarme's voice now rang with a false politeness. It dawned on me that he might take the food whether we gave it willingly or not. I cut my eyes in Elena's direction, and saw, from the periphery of my vision, how frightened she looked.

"You know," the gendarme said. "They don't pay us much for this job. It's hard getting by, if you know what I mean." He was looking at Roberto as he said this, his gold-toothed smile gleaming in the harsh sunlight.

"Sure," Roberto said. He got up and disappeared into their tent to fetch his wallet.

"You know," the young man continued, now turning to me. "I haven't seen my wife in three months. It gets pretty lonely up here."

When I looked at him I saw that his smile had turned ugly and diabolic. He adjusted his semi-automatic, and continued to sip his gourd of tea. I looked around me for some sort of weapon, but finding none, mentally prepared myself to jump him if he made any threatening or hostile moves.

The gendarme spat once, then wandered over to one of the piles of samples and poked at it with the muzzle of his rifle. "*Carajo*," he muttered, bending down to examine one of the enormous shark teeth. "I've never seen anything like this. Where did you find them?"

Elena appeared. She handed him a sack of rations. "We found them by a river about five kilometers east of here," she said, intimating that we'd found them on Argentine soil.

The gendarme gave an unbelieving smirk. He muttered something to himself and continued his prodding with the barrel of his semi-automatic.

Roberto returned and shook hands with the man, placing a wad of pesos in his hand. "Maybe this will help you out," he said, sarcastically.

"*Gracias*," the young man said, displaying his gold tooth. He kept looking down at the pile of shark teeth. "Could I have one of those?" he asked, pointing with the barrel of his gun.

"I'm afraid not," Roberto said. "Research, you know. If you like I can draw you a map of the place where you can find some more."

"But I thought you said you found these five kilometers east of here."

Roberto looked at me in surprise. He had been in the tent when Elena made had her comment, and now he realized that his own attempt to deflect the gendarme's suspicions had conflicted with an earlier fabrication. "Of course," he said. "You can't very well go tramping around on the Argentine side."

"The snows will be coming any day now," the young man said, turning his gaze to the peaks. "I don't mind if you stay in this valley until then. But I wouldn't come back if I were you. It looks dangerous here. You can see there's been a number of recent rock slides."

"We'll be leaving within that time frame," I assured him. "We're getting rather low on food ourselves."

The young man nodded. "I'll just pitch my tent over there, out of your way. I'll be gone in the morning. Thank you for the food, and for this," he said, holding up the wad of pesos.

"No problem," Roberto said, gritting his teeth and nodding with affected cordiality. "No problem at all."

The gendarme, true to his word, was gone the next morning. We slept late that day, having rested very little the night before. I had asked Elena if she wanted me to sleep in her tent that night, knowing that she'd feel safer with someone sleeping next to her. I later wondered if I hadn't just been taking advantage of the fact that she was afraid; but when she took me by the arm and said: "Stay with me, Antonio. That gendarme frightens me," I felt better about having asked her. Afterwards I continued to sleep in Elena's tent. Surprisingly, Roberto revealed no dismay with this arrangement, nor did he display any signs of jealousy or indignation. I shrugged this off, thinking maybe he had set his priorities and had found that the *Lagerstätten* was more important to him than Elena.

Three days later we were packed and heading out of the valley, our horses gasping and snorting under the heavy weights of our discoveries. The fact that we had left many of the fossils behind caused us a great deal of apprehension, especially as we were climbing back up the same pass that had led us into the valley and Elena noticed more tiny human specks on a saddle between two peaks on the Chilean side of the valley. "More gendarmes," she said. "They must be searching for their friend with the gold tooth."

Roberto turned his gaze to the border guards on the horizon, who were waiving in unison, obviously wanting to speak to us. "Don't worry," he said, waving back to the guards in an exaggerated manner. "They can't touch us now."

III.

Three weeks after our return to Buenos Aires, as the three of us sat in Roberto's office discussing a paper that we were to present to the Paleontological Congress in London, there came a knock at the door.

"Excuse me. Dr. Olivos?" said a bald, diminutive man with big lips and a double chin. He announced in a calm voice that his name was Colonel Santos. "May I sit down?" he asked politely.

"Sure. Sit down," Roberto said. His face betrayed an alarm at this strange visit. "What can I do for you, Colonel?"

The Colonel gave us a disarming smile, as if to put us at ease. "Something's come up regarding your expedition to the Andes," he said, "and I just wanted to go over a few things with you."

"What's this all about?" Roberto asked. He leaned back in his chair, nonchalantly, and tapped a pencil against the desk.

"The location of your discovery—" The Colonel pulled out a map. "Can you spot it for me?"

"Well. I'm not familiar with this map," Roberto said. "We used the Lagos surveys."

"Oh, yes. The Lagos surveys." He opened his briefcase and pulled out another set of maps. When the correct quadrant had been found, he spread the map out on the desk, and the four of us stood over it, glaring at it as if it were a treasure map.

"Can you point to the place?" the Colonel asked.

Roberto placed his finger in the steeply sided valley, denoted with a few tightly spaced contours on either side of the symbolic glacier. "Approximately here," he said.

"And how long were you there?" the Colonel asked. "From what dates, specifically."

Roberto hesitated. He tapped his pencil against the desk, as if this helped him to remember.

"From the twelfth of January to the eighteenth," Elena said. "Why? Is there something wrong?"

The Colonel ignored her question. "So. You were here in this valley. Were you aware that this is a disputed border region?" he asked innocuously.

"Yes. We knew that," I replied. "But according to the Lagos surveys we stayed on our side of the border. I understand that this is a contested area, but we felt we had some basis, given the circumstances, to continue our work there."

"We aren't aware of the specifics of the dispute — if that's what you mean," Elena said. "We met a Chilean border guard while we were there. He told us that we were in Chile, but he allowed us to stay."

"Yes, I was afraid of that," the Colonel said gloomily. "When did you meet this guard? On what day?"

"On the fifteenth of January," Roberto snapped. "Why is this so important?"

"I think it was the sixteenth," I said. "Not the fifteenth."

Roberto glared at me severely, as if to tell me to shut up.

"Maybe you were unaware of this," the Colonel said, his face retaining its gloominess, "but Chile and Argentina were in the process of settling our border disputes in that region. We were finally getting somewhere, after all these years of endless debates, finally agreeing to a proposed demarcation of our border. The only thing left to do was to sign the treaty, to put a few scribbles on a piece of paper, literally, for us to end this national headache. But now all that has changed."

"What are you getting at?" Elena asked in exasperation. "What exactly is all the trouble?"

"The trouble. Yes, well. There's quite a lot of that. The treaty has been nullified. And it looks as if our relations with the Chileans have been dealt a serious blow."

Colonel Santos slid a photograph onto Roberto's desk. It was a black and white image of a young man lying face-up in a depression in the ground, buried in a shallow grave of the fossiliferous *Lagerstätten*. There was a bloodstain on the man's shirt. His eyes were open slightly. His mouth was also open, revealing the familiar gold-toothed sneer of the gendarme.

"The Chileans read about your expedition in the newspapers," the Colonel said. "They claim you murdered this gendarme to protect the location of your discovery. They say you buried him in this grave and fled the mountains before they could reach you." He looked at us now with narrowed eyes, as if to glean the truth from our reactions. "They've officially requested your extradition," he continued. "They want to try you for murder."

The Colonel, of course, suspected us of a conspiracy. But I knew that he realized he had no proof of our guilt.

"We have declined, for now," he went on, "their request for extradition. The consensus is that you are the victims of a trumped up charge by the Chilean military, who blame you in order to sabotage the treaty." The Colonel rose to leave, and as he did so he looked each of us hard in the face, as if to satisfy himself, once and for all, of his judgment of us. I felt certain that he told his superiors that we had probably killed the gendarme, because subsequent to his visit, each of us was followed and watched closely by plainclothes policemen.

One day Colonel Santos called and invited me to meet him for lunch at a café on Florida Street. We sat at a table in the corner of the room. I noticed that he kept eyeing me curiously while he smoked cigarette after cigarette, drank cup after cup of black coffee, and chatted amiably, as if we were old friends. When I asked him why we were there, he stubbed out his cigarette and leaned back in his chair. "I understand," he said, "that your company has made an application to explore for minerals in a valley near the one where you found those fossils."

I admitted that this was true.

"Quite a coincidence, wouldn't you say?"

"I'm not sure what you mean by that, Colonel," I said.

"Well," he went on. "Up until now we suspected Roberto of killing the gendarme. But now, we're convinced that it was you, Antonio."

I laughed, and assured him that his suspicions were wrong. The Colonel continued to accuse me of killing the gendarme, though he was never menacing or threatening in his accusations.

"We've learned," he said, "that your company knew about the treaty all along, that they've been following it step by step over the last five years. They were opposed to the treaty because they knew that if the treaty were signed a large, potentially mineral-rich area would be conceded to Chile as part of the agreement. They lobbied us for months on this issue, and were becoming distressed when they saw that the treaty was nearing a conclusion. They made veiled threats to some of the negotiators. They offered them bribes. One of the congressmen involved told me that a woman showed up at his apartment one night, telling him that she was a gift from a wealthy friend. Still. None of these temptations worked, and so your bosses became desperate."

The Colonel paused to light another cigarette. "Then an opportunity arose," he said, arching his eyebrows and blowing smoke. "Your brother asked you to join him on an expedition that would take you into the heart of this disputed region. And so they sent you down there, hoping that you might corroborate the existence of minerals. Well. You found them, and now the treaty has been scuttled, and there will be no concessions of land to the Chileans. Quite a coincidence, wouldn't you say?"

"Are you here to thank me, Colonel, or to arrest me?"

"If it were up to me," he said, "I'd have you shot. But there are many in the government who are happy that things turned out the way they did. So. I suppose I am here to thank you."

The Colonel stood up and dropped some money on the table. "*Chau*, Antonio," he said, patting me on the shoulder as he walked toward the door. "Be careful you don't cross the border when you go digging for your minerals."

Los Penitentes

Above me the swirl of a lenticular cloud showered snow crystals off the face of the volcanic massif. I arose, and put on my headlamp. Slowly, painfully, I moved along the axis of a narrow arête, kick-stepping my way down the knife-edge ridge with anchoring stabs of my ice ax. Images of my fall filtered through my mind as I trudged through the snow: the chaos of sliding down the ice; the blur of a looming outcrop; the interlude of lost consciousness and the panic that gripped me as I awoke and realized that I was unable to breathe. For a time I lay in the snow, unable to move. We feared the worst, and so my guide, Rodrigo, made a quick retreat to our base camp to gather our gear and return to my location to make a higher camp. As darkness enveloped the eastern slopes and a bitter cold set in, I slowly regained my sense of self, as well as my confidence that all was not lost. Within an hour I was up on my feet, bloodied and bruised, but with all my bones intact.

Ignoring the pain as best I could, I inched my way down the slopes of this unnamed Andean peak, exhausted, dehydrated, dazed with hypoxia. My lungs gurgled with the telltale sounds of high altitude pulmonary edema, morosely referred to as "The Death Rattle" by many climbers. I zigzagged back and forth, calling out to my Argentine companion, unsure if the voice I heard was even real or if my attempts at echolocation were successful.

As I approached the snow-covered trough which separated the pinnacle that we had just summitted from its lower elevation twin, I saw in my headlamp, not ten meters below me, the slouched figure of Rodrigo Alvarez. He stepped toward me, his arms outstretched, his eyes shut tightly and his face covered in crusts of ice.

"Gringo, are you there?" he cried, calling me by the nickname he had christened me with early in our trek. "Is that you?"

I grabbed him by the arm and we held on to each other to steady ourselves against the wind, slapping each other on the back as if to reassure ourselves that we were not alone any longer, that we were now a team once again. As I shone the light on his face, I could see that Rodrigo was not the man who had left me only a few hours before. His eyes were ice-encrusted slits, his cheeks swollen and frostbitten.

"My God. What happened to you?"

"It's my eyes," he cried back. "I can't open them anymore. I've gone snow-blind." He gave me a short, demented little laugh, as if Nature's cruel joke required from him this pathetic response. "It's my own stupid fault, Gringo. My sunglasses — I don't know what happened to them. And I did not have my extra pair with me."

"I'll try the radio again," I said. No one had responded to our radio calls since we had entered the valley, and no one answered them now. We had set out from Mendoza one week earlier, eight of us in all: three from the States, one from Europe, and a couple from New Zealand, plus our two Argentine guides. All of the expedition clients, with the sole exception of myself, had gotten sick from either dysentery or the altitude; and so the other guide, Julio was his name, took them out. I insisted on pushing ahead. Rodrigo tried to talk me out of this, but I felt perfectly fine and had no inclination to turn back when so much effort, not to mention money, had already been invested.

Fortunately Rodrigo's journey back to base camp had been productive. He carried with him our tent, sleeping bags, the stove and some food and water. I relieved him of this gear, and within an hour I had our new camp laid out, tucked snugly between a cliff overhang and a long wedge of rock formation that had sloughed off from the outcropping, leaving an open space beneath. We lay in our tent and warmed our hands against the blue flames of the propane gas stove, spooning from our food packages little steaming mounds of re-hydrated rice and chicken chunks. It was delicious. We were alive, battered and exhausted, but alive. We now had nourishment, and shelter from the bitter cold. We had a long way to go yet, but our immediate needs had been met, and we had won some additional time to consider our next steps.

Rodrigo's blindness concerned me greatly. I'd seen this affliction in other climbers, and knew it often took days to heal. "Listen to me, Gringo," he said, taking hold of my arm, "I won't be able to guide you any further. It is you who will have to lead us out of this place. Do you understand me? You are the guide now. It's up to you to lead us back home."

No problema. Yo me encargo de todo, I said to him. "No problem. I'll take care of everything."

That night I dreamt that I had fallen into a lake. The water was crystal clear and I could see everything around me perfectly. There were people sitting around a table nearby, their mouths expelling air bubbles with "Death Rattle" noises as they conversed with one another. One of the players was showing off his skill by shuffling a deck of cards from one hand to the other, each card floating slowly across the aqueous medium in perfect, continuous momentum, until it smoothly met its place amongst the other cards. The shuffler kept looking over at me as he performed his trick, as if waiting for some action on my part. I noticed an empty chair beside him and understood at once that this seat at the table was meant for me. Imbued now with a kind of *a priori* knowledge that only dreams can reveal, immersed in surreality, I knew that the card players were waiting for me to drown so that I could join them in a game of cribbage. I heard the feverish pounding of my heart grow louder, and as I struggled to hold on to the last vapors of my breath I saw that the players were now laughing at me, as if they found my fight for survival frivolous and amusing.

I did not join the card players in their game of cribbage, however. Instead I found myself awake, conscious, cognizant of the fact that I was in severe distress. *I was struggling for breath.*

Something held me down, enveloped me, smothered me. I panicked and punched upwards against the tent, which now pressed flat against my face, compressed by the weight of several feet of snow. "Rodrigo!" I cried. "Wake up! We've got to get out!" Somehow my mind grasped that an avalanche now entombed us. I pushed outward again, and found that the snow gave way more easily this time. Again and again I plowed, thrashing my arms forward, until enough space was produced to allow me to unzip the tent and pierce through the fan of snow into the open air above. Luck had favored us, for the overhanging rock that we had pitched our tent under had provided enough structural enforcement to prevent a complete and total burial.

Rodrigo came to. "I'm ok. I'm ok," he assured me, upon regaining his composure. "But I can't breathe very well. We need to get out of here quickly."

We extricated ourselves from the pack of snow, which I figured to be about six feet in depth, until finally we stood free and clear on the surface. The sun broke over the line of jagged peaks, showering us with orange light rays. Far below, swathed in purple shadows, we could see the enormous glacier fanning out onto the lowermost slopes, spilling its wrinkled, deltaic form onto the valley floor.

We gathered up our gear, ate a few mouthfuls of trail mix, and began our descent, one short step at a time, Rodrigo with his arm around my neck. His eyes were still swollen completely shut, but there was little I could do to help him.

"How are your eyes now?" I asked, as we trudged slowly downhill.

"Like someone is sticking knives into them," he said, attempting to smile.

Ojalá que se pongan bien pronto, I said. "Hopefully they will put themselves right soon."

"Your Spanish is not so bad, Gringo," he said sleepily. "Did I tell you that already?"

"Yes, you told me that once."

"And what about your woman?" he asked, drifting to his next thought. "Do you get along well with her?"

"Yes, I do," I said. "Very well."

He smiled. "That is good. Maybe you have learned that a man and a woman need to accept their differences, and love each other in spite of them. My Maria is always there for me; sometimes she wants to change me in ways that don't suit me, but we are learning to understand each other over time. We need to get back to our loved ones, Gringo. They are counting on us. Tell me. What do you see now?"

"I see the glacier below us, a few miles away. At the rate we're going we won't reach it until nightfall. The weather appears to be clearing up to the east. Maybe we'll get a rest from all this snow."

"We must pick up the rest of our cache. I couldn't carry everything up by myself. There is more food there. More warm clothes. And more medicine."

"*Sí. De acuerdo.*"

"Don't forget," he said. "You are the guide now. That is a big responsibility."

"Yes," I replied. "I will lead us out of this place."

As we headed down the mountain, Rodrigo began to sing a tango by Carlos Gardel called *Volver* (Return). I was familiar with the song — it surprised him that a foreigner would know this — and he taught me the words in Spanish so that we could sing it together on our way down the mountain. In English the words roughly translate to the following. My crude translation will not do it justice.

I make out the flickering
Of the lights in the distance
That mark my return.
They're the same ones that lit up,
With their pallid reflections,
Deep hours of pain.
And although I never wanted to return,
One always returns
To one's first love.
The quiet street where the echo said:
Yours is her life, yours is her love
Beneath the mocking look of the stars
Today with indifference sees me return.

At the end of ten hours we found ourselves standing at an elevation of eighteen thousand three hundred feet, at the head of the main glacial tributary, the largest of multiple arms of snaking ice fields conjoined into an amorphous sheet in the valley below, eventually dissipating into a lake formed from the terminus of glacial moraine. We set up camp on a level spot by a stream, overlooking an incredible view of the field of blue ice and snow. *Bergshrunds*, gaping crevasses, cut across the glacier like open knife wounds. The expanse of the glacier was tremendous; it seemed to stretch for miles on end, and there was no getting around its massive core.

We had picked up the remainder of our gear; now the task ahead of us was to cross the glacier, find the trail on the other side of the valley, and head downstream until we met with the main highway. From there we would hitch a ride to the small village populated with mule drivers and local guides who offered their services to the incoming expeditions. We longed to get back to this poor, indigenous community — this sleepy outpost of the Cordillera — to recuperate from the ravages of the wild with alternating bouts of sleep, drunkenness, and gluttony, after which, our spirits then fully rejuvenated, we would step aboard the decrepit, coughing *omnibus* and wind our way back down to the city of Mendoza.

* * *

The sun quickly disappeared, casting its last rays over the snow-capped peaks that now glistened in the approaching dusk. A pale half-moon hung yellow behind a misting cloud. Stars lit the deepness of space with radiant points. The solitude of this place, once beautiful and pristine, now felt godless and unforgiving. As I lay in my bag, listening to the wind whip the tent flaps, the Death Rattle grew louder, my chest heaving for every breath, the gurgling now deeper in my lungs. I took Diamox to help improve my breathing. Rodrigo, for his part, struggled throughout the night with his own afflictions. He awoke from his sleep at two in the morning, screaming in agony as the corneas of his eyes formed blisters. I gave him some oxycodone, and he finally fell asleep.

The next morning we awoke at the crack of dawn, cold, tired, exhausted. I patched up Rodrigo's eyes with some gauze to prevent any light from entering his field of vision. Then we ate some hot oatmeal, and discussed our upcoming traverse.

"From the way you have described our surroundings," Rodrigo said, "I believe we may be much farther north than we should be. Tell me what you see now."

I described to him the valley of ice that lay before us, the huge spikes of ice that jutted out of the snow like an endless cultivation of stalagmites; the distances of the other branching glaciers that flowed down from the nearby ranges; and I gave descriptions and bearings of the surrounding landmark peaks, including a bearing on

Aconcagua, the highest peak in the Andes. Finally, I spotted our location on the topographic map with the lat-long coordinates provided by the GPS handheld. In short, the orientation confirmed his suspicion that we were a few miles farther north from the track we had taken during our arrival.

"Ok," he said. "How are you feeling?"

I told him not so good.

"Can you walk?"

I told him yes.

"Then," he said, "we'll make our way across the glacier, heading east through the penitentes. It's the shortest way out of here. We can gain at least a day if we go that route. It's slow going, and dangerous, but it will save us precious time in the long run."

Sí. Lo vamos a lograr, I said. "Yes. We will succeed."

With his hand on my shoulder, and each of us tethered to the other with rope, we struck out onto the field of ice and snow, into the field of the penitentes. We carefully wound our way through the giant shards of ice that protruded from the floor of the glacier, eight to nine feet high, standing like sun-sculpted spears. These oddities of nature, formed by a process called sublimation whereby ice is melted directly into water vapor by the powerful rays of the sun, are common in the Andes. They provoked in me both a sense of awe and trepidation, especially as we penetrated deeper into the shadowy forest of ice, their delicate and fragile stalks surrounding us with an eerie majesty.

After three hours of walking we stopped for a short rest.

"What do you see?" Rodrigo asked.

"Just a lot of ice," I replied. "There seems to be no end to it."

"What does the GPS tell us?"

"Shit. I forgot to turn on the GPS and take waypoints of our track."

"Never mind," he said. "Just turn it on now and mark our location. You should be able to see our current location in relation to the lower base camp."

I pressed the "On" button, but the unit did not power up. "Must be the batteries," I said. "I'll replace them." But this did not work either; the replacement batteries were also dead. The cold had drained them all.

"We'll have to navigate the old fashioned way," I told him. And I suddenly felt an incapacitating fear gripping my guts. I had only a vague idea where we were, even less in what direction we needed to go. It struck me that this foray into the labyrinth of ice had been an incredibly bad choice, and I flatly told him so. "Look. I'm not familiar with this terrain like you are," I said. "In fact, I have no idea if we are going in the right direction. Maybe we should turn back."

"No!" he snapped. "We can't turn back now. We've gone too far."

"So what do we do? Just keep going and hope for the best? That doesn't seem like a very good plan to me."

"What the hell happened to you, Gringo?" he retorted. "What happened to all of that Yankee optimism of yours? 'Take it easy,' you always say. 'Don't be afraid'. 'We're going to succeed.' Was that all just a bunch of bullshit? I think maybe it was. Tell me. Why the hell did you come down here anyway?"

I considered his question for a few moments. "I came here to test myself," I said. "To see if I have what it takes to conquer this peak. There may be other reasons, less obvious than those."

"Oh? And what might those be?"

"The penitentes gave me the clue," I said.

"What? I don't understand you. Maybe you need to lie down."

"No, I'm ok. I'm not going to tell you that everything is going to be fine — I really don't know if it will or not. We may die in this place, but then that's not a surprise. We knew that was a possibility even before we came here."

Rodrigo faced me, blind, frostbitten, his head wrapped in gauze. He said nothing.

"It turns out that the word penitentes has another meaning," I told him. "I knew I'd heard this word somewhere before, then it came to me as we wandered through this ice field. I remembered that years ago I had learned about a religious group called the Penitentes. I heard about them on a visit to a very old adobe church in northern New Mexico, out in the middle of nowhere. It was built over three hundred years ago by the early Spanish settlers, shortly after the founding of Santa Fe. One of the priests of this church asked me if I'd like to visit a nearby Morada, which is an adobe house where the Penitentes meet and worship. He explained that the Penitente Brotherhood was a little known, pseudo-secret sect, at one time vigorously suppressed by the Catholic church, that traced it origins back to Europe during the Middle Ages. They believe that sin is purged from the soul through physical suffering, just as Christ himself suffered on the cross for the sake of our sins, and that forgiveness comes to those who willingly inflict pain on themselves to emulate the suffering and sacrifice of Christ."

"I think I have heard of this," Rodrigo said. "Aren't they the ones who whip themselves?"

"Yes, the same," I replied. "I told the priest I would like to see what he was talking about, and he escorted me two miles down a deserted road to the Morada. It was a very small adobe structure, a single room with an altar and a few benches. The priest told me that the sect had survived for over two hundred years in the Rio Grande valley, and that they still carried out their secret purification rituals in spite of the disdain most people have for this practice. As we approached the Morada on foot, we could see through a small window that there were people inside. This made the priest nervous. He told me we had to leave right away, that there was a ritual in progress."

"What were they doing? Were they beating themselves?"

"Yes. Some of the men had their shirts off. Their backs were bloodied from the whip. By then the priest had run off, but I stayed and watched as they chanted and self-flagellated with a rope that held the head of a prickly cactus lashed to the end of it. Naturally, I was sickened by this display, so I turned to go and found myself confronted by an old, wrinkled Indian woman wrapped in a shawl. She just stood there glaring at me, as if demanding me to account for my presence there.

"Just then a procession came up the hill. It was a reenactment of the crucifixion. The old lady scurried away to participate in it, so when she left I was able to watch the entire ritual. They roped a half-naked man to a large wooden cross and stuck the cross in a hole in the ground, just like they did with Jesus."

Rodrigo grew silent, as if this tale had struck a personal note with him. "So," he said. "You think that what you are doing now is the same thing as those Penitentes."

"In a way, yes. I couldn't tell you specifically what I'm trying to atone for. Maybe it's for everything I've ever done wrong in my life."

"Well, Gringo," he said, with a measure of understanding. "I suppose we all have our crosses to bear. But I really don't think you are purposely punishing yourself on this trip to atone for your past sins, whatever they may be. I think some bad shit is happening to us up here. Nothing more. Nothing less. There is no ritual behind it. Only bad fucking luck. *Entendés?*"

"I'm sure you're right," I said. "But I can't help but wonder at the parallels. Perhaps my penitence is less directed than theirs."

"*No te hagas problemas*, Gringo." He smiled at his own advice not to make problems for myself, playfully mocking my own inane platitudes.

"Maybe those Penitentes need to get laid more often," he said, reflectively. "You'd be amazed how swiftly screwing can cure a damaged soul." He produced a belly laugh that made me laugh along with him until a fit of coughing overwhelmed me.

"Let's go," I said. "*Vamos a tener éxito.*"

We walked for another two hours, finally emerging from the field of penitentes into a flat and open snowfield atop the glacier. We had a quick lunch of dried fruit and nuts, all the while beaming with happiness at having successfully emerged from the ice maze. As we reshouldered our packs and headed down, we were excited to see, a few miles in the distance, on the other side of the glacier, the winding trail that would soon carry us back to civilization.

"Tell me what you see," Rodrigo said, and as I described to him the landscape, he nodded confidently and said that we were indeed on the right track. "Three days from now we'll be sitting comfortably on a bus, heading back to Mendoza," he said.

As we crossed the glacial plain, I suddenly felt the snow give way beneath my feet and I plummeted feet first into a gaping crevasse, the rope tightening momentarily as my weight pulled on it, wrenching all the breath from my lungs. The rope slackened again as Rodrigo came tumbling behind me, smashing against the crevasse walls with hard thuds and muffled cries of pain. We tumbled this way for what seemed like minutes, though it could not have been more than a few seconds at most. Finally I came to a rest on a level spot, fifty or so feet below the surface. I called out to

Rodrigo, but got no answer. He had fallen farther down into the crevasse than I — the rope that had connected us had come undone on his end, and I could not see where he was in the darkness below. I kept very quiet in an effort to locate a sign, a noise that would indicate he was alive and where he was, but no noises arose from the abyss, despite my repeated calls over the ensuing minutes and hours.

* * *

It took me two days to pull myself out of the crevasse. Amazingly, no bones had broken during my fall, though I had many contusions and a banged up knee. All my efforts to locate Rodrigo had failed. He was either dead or unconscious, and while I held out hope for the latter, in my condition I was at a loss to prove it. Even if I had found him, I did not have the strength to lift him out by myself, and was uncertain at the time whether I had the strength even to pull myself out. Using my ice ax, I inched my way up out of the darkness, methodically carving out foot and hand holds, taking my time to ensure my strength did not run out, always paranoid of slipping and falling back down even deeper into the ice. When I finally reached the surface, blinded by the strong reflections of light off the newly fallen snow, I was hugely relieved to find an expedition of ten climbers heading up the valley to summit one of the high peaks in the area. They were no more than tiny specks when I first saw them, but little by little their forms grew in size, and with shouts and waves I managed to draw their attention and let them know that I needed help.

The expedition leader, an Argentine named Enrique from Mendoza, knew Rodrigo well. "We have been in radio contact with your outfit," he said. "They asked us to keep an eye out for you." While others in the group fixed a rope and rappelled down into the crevasse to look for Rodrigo, Enrique called in to the guide company headquarters in

Mendoza and relayed the bad news. "There is still hope," he told me, resting his hand sympathetically on my shoulder. "Rodrigo is one tough son of a bitch." "Yes," I told him, *Lo vamos a encontrar bien*, I said. "We are going to find him in good shape." But when they finally located and retrieved his body, there were no signs of life, and no response to our attempts to resuscitate him. My guide, Rodrigo Alvarez, was dead.

* * *

The funeral took place only a day after his body arrived in Mendoza. He was laid to rest in a small cemetery on the outskirts of town, adjacent to a large vineyard. All his family and friends, who numbered in the hundreds, showed up to pay their respects. Dressed in black, covered in veils, they looked at me with stony faces; some with menacing, vengeful scowls; others with masks of incomprehension, as if they wanted me to provide an explanation of some kind but were unsure how to ask for it. I spoke with his wife, Maria, a strikingly pretty young woman, soft-spoken, but clearly possessed of a strong character. I told her how often he spoke of her during our trek, how much he professed his love for her. She smiled a little when I told her this, happy to know that his thoughts were with her. She thanked me for coming to the funeral. "I also want to thank you," she said, "for sticking by Rodrigo to the very end. I always told him this job was far too dangerous, but he said he was doing it to save money for us to buy a house. It was a burden I told him not to carry. He knew it worried me to no end. But he will carry that cross no more, for my Rodrigo now climbs with the angels."

Now that I am home, and have written of these events, I no longer question the lessons of this pilgrimage. Instead I sing in fond remembrance the verses of *Volver* — and raise a glass of the Mendozan wine that I carried home with me, grown from the land in which he lies, in honor of my brave and worthy comrade. An exquisite cabernet, and aptly labeled too; for it is named for those strange and wonderful Andean ice forms sculpted by showers of the suns' UV rays – named as well, perhaps, for the tormented believers who purge their sins with self-inflicted wounds: *Los Penitentes.*

The Human Cry

One cold day in May of 1978, as meandering rivers of impatient Portenians flooded the streets and avenues of downtown Buenos Aires, she emerged from the crowd, bundled in a woolen scarf and heavy tweed coat. She moved swiftly down Corrientes Avenue, past the lampposts and unshuttered shop windows, through the billowing exhaust fumes of diesel microbuses and taxis, penetrating the smoke of the street vendor fires and the wafting smell of roasting walnuts. She was that perfect blend of the Old and New Worlds, with dark, penetrating eyes, a slender figure, and espresso-colored hair that fell suantly over her shoulders. A smile lit her face as a young *pibe* standing by a bus stop bench caught sight of her and attempted to make conversation by throwing her street pick-up lines, those ridiculous mating calls we affectionately refer to as *piropos*. She shook her head at him, still with a smile, and continued down the street.

"Her name is Alejandra," Lucho told me. "She's the owner of the printing shop on Montevideo."

We were sitting in the *El Colonial* hotel restaurant, our table next to a large window facing the street, eating American style breakfast and reading the newspaper, watching for the movements of the woman called Alejandra.

"What do we know about her?" I asked.

"Not much. Her family is from the province of *Santiago del Estero*. She came here to attend the university, and later obtained a graduate degree in the United States in Political Science."

"She is beautiful," I said, a bit too wistfully.

From the look on his face, Lucho was annoyed by the inofficiousness of my remark. He threw some *efectivo* on the table, motioning for me to contribute my part to the bill. "Come on," he said, peering out the window. "She's heading into her shop now. I see two other men entering as well, just behind her."

We left the restaurant and scurried across the street. At the next intersection we came to a stop by a galleria entrance in order to surveil the printing shop and size up any potentially threatening activity within.

"Ok," Lucho said, gazing around him. "Our cover story is that we work for a book publisher by the name of *Proverbio*, and that we are here to ask about their services. Once inside we'll look for signs of contraband."

The shop stood on the second floor of a whitewashed cinder block building decorated with the usual graffiti condemning the military. A large sign with a painting of a compass hung above the door, with bright red letters proclaiming the name of the business: Compass Printing.

We entered the first floor, which was empty, save for a few sawhorses, piles of wooden planks and cans of unopened paint. The windows had been painted, allowing a dirty pale glow to enter the room. We mounted the stairs near the front door and found ourselves in a dark, narrow hallway that smelled of dust. A door with our suspect's company name painted in black letters stood before us.

A throaty, nicotine-cured male voice called out over the intercom: "Good morning. Please state your business."

"Good morning," Lucho replied. "My associate and I would like to discuss your printing services. Our publishing company will be producing a small circulation magazine and would like to know what your rates are."

A long silence ensued. Finally we heard the voice clear its throat, and say: "What did you say was the name of your company?"

"We work for a small publishing house called *Proverbio*. Can you let us in to discuss obtaining a quote?"

A few moments passed, then the voice of a woman announced: "Please excuse us. We've been under a tight deadline on several projects and may not be able take on any more orders until our backlog is cleared. But please step inside and we will discuss your needs."

The buzzer went off. The door release clicked. We entered the room and found ourselves in a large workshop with several printing machines clanking in the back. There was a counter at the front with posters tacked onto a wall illustrating numerous book and magazine covers. To the side was an old fashioned desk, the kind with the roll up cover and numerous little cubby holes stuffed with unpaid bills, as well as a few other flat work tables arranged by the window, each occupied by a draftsman or designer who cut and arranged printed sheets or worked on book bindings. Rows of boxes stood stacked against the walls, marked with titles and shipment locations. I counted six people altogether, four in the front, and two in the back working the presses.

Alejandra greeted us at the counter. She did not smile as we approached and made conscious efforts not to look at us directly for too long, instead throwing us short little glances, first to Lucho and then to me, before looking off towards the binders or down at her hands. She was as pretty up close as I had imagined her from afar, but I kept my thoughts to the purpose at hand.

Lucho bypassed our little ruse and went straight to the point.

"Are you the owner of this place?"

"Yes, I am."

"What is your name, miss?"

"Alejandra Vicente."

"We have reports that you are printing anti-government propaganda from this location. Is that true?"

"No, it is not," she exclaimed, her dark eyes flashing in anger. "We do not allow that here."

Lucho motioned for me to follow him. "We will have to search all of that," he said, pointing to the rows of boxes. Upon reaching the wall he grabbed one of the boxes and swiped it to the floor.

The woman turned to her companions in the back of the room and the two men came rushing towards us, pulling pistols from behind their shirts.

I remember seeing Lucho reach to his waist to pull out his semi-automatic; how he struggled to move his jacket out of the way to reach the gun handle. Before I could pull my own weapon, a shot rang out.

Lucho fell to the floor, bleeding profusely from the neck.

I ran to him without thinking — such was my poor training at that point. I stood over him, watching helplessly as his eyes rolled back into his head, as he exhaled his last breath, rolled his head to the side, and quietly died.

A hard blow knocked me out.

* * *

I awoke in a small storage room lined with shelves stacked with newly printed paperback books. I was laid out on a cot, my left hand cuffed to the radiator piping on the wall. Above me a cracked window covered with chicken wire let in a dingy light.

"How long have you two been following me?" Alejandra asked. She was sitting on the edge of my cot, smoking a cigarette.

"Not long. A few days."

She looked towards the door, as if she were about to call one of her associates to join her in the room, but instead looked down at the floor, nervously flicking the ash of her cigarette.

"I'm sorry about your partner," she said.

"I'll be sure to put that on his epitaph. Here lies Lucho Sanchez, killed by a terrorist who claimed she was sorry."

She looked at me with anger in her eyes, but said nothing.

"Where am I?" I demanded to know.

"Somewhere safe. We shut down everything and moved before the rest of your death squad could show up."

"Do you have any idea what they will do to you for this?"

"Yes. I was a prisoner for over six months at your torture center at *Campo de Mayo*."

She looked keenly into my eyes, as if to judge the impact this admission would have on me. "Maybe you should put this on your friend's epitaph: Here lies Lucho Sanchez, killed in the act of censuring the press."

She handed me her pack of cigarettes and a box of matches, and left me alone to wonder if I would ever leave that place alive.

* * *

The days passed slowly. I was given plenty to eat, and was provided many conveniences to make my stay seem less like imprisonment: a feather pillow, two woolen blankets, a radio — which I used religiously to listen to the ongoing World Cup matches, hosted in that year by Argentina — and, of course, the library of leftist books and revolutionary pamphlets.

One day Alejandra came into my room and threw me a bar of chocolate. "You strike me as someone with a sweet tooth," she said.

The next day she returned bearing other gifts: a razor, shaving cream, a clean T-shirt, and a bag of *empanadas*.

"How is my follower today?" she asked, using the English word that could either mean 'pursuer' (*perseguidor*) or 'supporter' (*partidario*).

I shot her a puzzled look.

"You followed me. That was your job. Was it not?"

"Yes. I suppose that's why they wanted to train me, to be very good at following people." I bristled at this absurdity. "Thank you for these things."

"I see you've been reading some of our literature." She pointed to an overturned copy of one of Marx's publications entitled, "The Poverty of Philosophy".

"Yes," I admitted. "Marx and Engels I find interesting. But some of this other shit is so badly written that it compromises its own credibility."

I expected a caustic reply to this criticism, especially since some of the work I was referring to had actually been written by her; but I was instead surprised when she pursed her lips together and gave a slight nod, as if she agreed with what I had said and was pondering the implications of this.

"Finish your Marx," she said. "Tomorrow I want you to read something for me, something a bit more up to date. We're drafting a work that we think will help make a difference. But I need someone to proofread it before we go to print, someone with a modicum of literary intelligence, which none of my partners seem to have."

"And why in God's name would I help you?"

"Because if you do, I'll let you go. And who knows, Marcos, maybe God will forgive you for making life hell for so many people. But if you refuse to help I may not be able to stop them from taking your life. Many of them have family and friends that have vanished."

The next day she brought me a typed first draft manuscript of the now well-known political treatise entitled *El Grito Humano* (The Human Cry), by Alejandra Vicente. That this work on the oppressed in Latin America — a blistering document on the treatment of the politically active by both democratic and military governments — was to become as famous a statement on injustice as Martin Luther King's "Letter from a Birmingham Jail" is irrefutable. The fact that we spent days going over its contents together, reading over passages into the early morning hours, filling ashtrays with Marlboro cigarettes and drinking gourd after gourd of bitter *mate* tea: editing, correcting, deleting, refining, clarifying, is, I would venture to say, unthinkable. That she incorporated nearly all of my suggested edits and recommendations to solidify her arguments by improving the structure of her rhetoric, is a fact that history, other than what is documented in this chronicle, does not record. And so it came to pass that I served as the de facto editor of the outlawed *El Grito Humano*, contributing, in my own small way, to making Alejandra's passionate words a rallying cry for a silent revolution in the minds of those who read it.

* * *

Alejandra drove me in her car to my apartment, not far from the *Teatro Colón*. It was a glorious day, for me especially, but also for Argentina. Not only had I just been released from my captivity, it was on this very day — in fact during the same hour of my release — that Argentina beat the Netherlands 3-1 to win the 1978 FIFA World Cup. The streets quickly filled with honking cars and trucks, people spilling out of their apartments, out of the shops, restaurants and bars, running pell-mell along the avenues, screaming wildly at the top of their lungs, waving the Argentine flag and pouring beer over each other, embracing total strangers with brotherly affection, as if we did not live in the midst of a Dirty War that ravaged the very foundation of our society — dancing in the streets with joyous abandon, as though the world had just been saved from annihilation by the hand of a vengeful God.

"We need to celebrate and feel good about ourselves," Alejandra observed. "I just hope that one day we'll find everyone shouting in the streets again, celebrating an end to all the chaos and violence. When that day comes, you won't have to follow people like me anymore. Take care, Marcos. I won't forget you." She kissed me on the cheek, and pulled away from the crowds in her rasping Citroen. We never saw each other again.

* * *

I will not go into all the sordid details of my debriefing. I told my superiors the facts as I knew them, and pleaded ignorance of my captor's conspiracies and the location of their hideouts. But then, one day, several months later, everything changed for the worse. I was taken to an interrogation room and pressed hard for more details on my relationship with Alejandra. How long did I know her before my so-called kidnapping, they asked. Oh, they said, we are well aware of your collaboration with these Montonero terrorists. The tiny concrete room soon filled with military uniforms. It was clear that they possessed intelligence suggesting my capture was not entirely as I had described it. One of the uniforms tossed a book on the table, and said: "Your comrade Alejandra was shot dead yesterday, Marcos. We found this on her." It was, of course, a first edition copy of *El Grito Humano*. I looked up at them, feigning innocence and confusion.

"Open it," the uniform commanded. "Look at the dedication. We know that you helped produce this piece of trash."

There, on the second page, at the top, in English, was written the words:

To my follower, Marcos, whose intelligence has furthered the cause of justice.

"My follower!" I yelled, recalling the double meaning of this word. "Yes. I did follow her. Lucho and I — we tailed her like you asked us to. But I was not in allegiance with her! I gave her no intelligence!"

The uniforms encircled me. They cursed at me and struck me with their fists, then hauled me off to a secret detention center called *La ESMA (Escuela Superior de Mecánica de la Armada)*, a stygian place of lost souls whose cries of pain and pleas for mercy would go unanswered for the next five years.

Shortly thereafter, the electric shocks began, and I began my descent into the hell that thousands of others had visited before me.

El Nevado de Cachi

I sat on the porch of my adobe house, watching the parrots fly low over the gravelly banks of the Calchaquí River. The river coursed quietly between cobbled channels, little more than trickling rivulets. Behind its banks rose the snow-capped massif — El Nevado de Cachi — ascending into the sky like an archangel, casting plum-colored shadows against its runnelled slopes and dominating the arid landscape with earthen majesty.

I lived just down the road from a pre-Incan archeological site where my ancestors, the Diaguita, once lived. From my porch I would sometimes see the young woman who ran the site. She wandered amongst the excavated holes in the ground, patiently explaining to random curiosity seekers how my ancestors, when not embroiled in tribal warfare, had studied the arts of healing and magic, sacrificing, when necessity demanded it, their children in desperate appeals to the mother god, Pachamama. "Marauders stormed into the valley five hundred years ago," avowed the archeologist's pamphlet, which every visitor received, "making slaves of the Diaguita. First came the Inca from the north, extending their empire to its southernmost limit. The Spanish arrived soon afterwards, and quickly subjugated the local population with civil and religious mandates." In spite of these hostilities our cultures managed to converge, and the people of this valley, isolated by the vastness of the Puna plateau and flanked by the high peaks of Cachi, spent their days farming the land and herding llama to subsist in the beautiful but harsh environment.

My house was constructed in the mixed colonial and native style, with a base of river cobbles, walls of adobe bricks covered with cracked plaster, and dark green doors topped with heavy supporting planks. Twisted iron bars covered the open windows. A roof of wood slats, topped with a thick layer of mud, painted long brown streaks down the walls with the sporadic summer rains. I had built my home in 1973, shortly after selling the farm. I was young and strong in those days, newly married to the best friend of my younger sister, Josephina. My young wife, Beatriz, had been a quiet soul. She bore us four children without complaint, and raised them while working tirelessly as a maid for one of the landowners who kept a large estancia on the edge of town. She was a small woman, barely five feet tall — I can see her now, covered in a multi-colored alpaca shaw — and I never once regretted asking her to marry me.

In those early days of our marriage we had still been tied to the land, living on a few hectares of riverfront that had been passed down to me by my uncle. Things had gone well for a time. Along with our neighbors, we lived well off the land, raising chickens, goats, maize, quinoa, and potatoes. There was no shortage of food or money. Water was plentiful. The crop was bountiful, the animals healthy and reproducing. And yet, one fall season when the winds blew dust through the town in swirls, our good fortune came abruptly to an end, as if the gods had suddenly damned us. A dark and ominous shadow crept stealthily into our lives, unfolding one misfortune after another. What little rain that fell in the region eventually ceased. The snow stopped falling on the mountains and the intricate network of irrigation ditches dug by our ancestors soon ran dry. Only a gouged out channel of gravel remained — a long and sinuous drainage highway stretching for miles through the high desert valley. Even the tall cactus that grew by the thousands along the hillsides began to die off, their up-turned arms turned yellow and sagging. The goats, once numerous and surrounded by lively kids, grew sickly and produced little milk. The llama and vicuña became harder to find. And with the harvest growing smaller every year, many abandoned the village of Cachi altogether and headed for the cities — to Salta or Jujuy or La Rioja; some even as far as Buenos Aires. The cemetery on the top of the hill overlooking the village, lined with the stick crosses of the poor, welcomed ever more visitors in those hard days.

One day in the summer of 1982, my youngest daughter, Amelia, only seven years old at the time, disappeared. She had been playing with a stray dog by the side of the road, and when we called her in for dinner she did not answer. In panic we searched along the road, amongst the hills, across the fields, along the riverbed and on every street and playground in town. There was never any trace of her. Not one person had seen her after she'd gone missing. For days the Cachi police put out bulletins and "missing" posters and patrolled the neighborhood streets and back alleys, but they never found any leads. Stories of loved ones disappearing were not uncommon in those days — rumors of suspected anarchists picked up by the military in the neighborhoods of towns and cities. But what could a little girl in a remote village have to do with any of this? No. She simply vanished, my only daughter! And when finally we admitted to ourselves that Amelia was gone, we reluctantly gave up our fruitless searches, and lived in darkness for the next twenty years.

Shortly after Amelia disappeared, Beatriz succumbed to her own misery and died; though, according to Dr. Sanchez, it was a tumor that ended her life. My three remaining children grew up and moved away. One went to college in Cordoba. The others found jobs outside of the province. As the years progressed, I found it more difficult to support myself; my life-long pursuit of becoming a well-read, self-educated man remained an honorable yet profitless interest. For a time I worked the maize fields or herded the guanaco of the landowner that Beatriz had once worked for. I harvested Malbec and Carbernet grapes and assisted with the winemaking operations in one of the regional bodegas. To earn a few extra pesos I made clay figurines of llamas — exact replicas of the one I'd once made for Amelia — selling them to tourists and artesania shop owners in the Cachi town square. Through the connections of a friend I found work as a guide for a man named Carlos Palmero, a local outfitter who led climbing expeditions to the high altitude summits of El Nevado de Cachi range. At sixty-two years of age, I began to wonder how much energy I had left for such strenuous endeavors.

As I watched the sun slowly slip behind the mountains, a familiar rev of a truck engine caught my attention. It was Carlos Palmero. He turned a corner in his green Toyota four-wheel drive and pulled into my drive. Carlos was a tall, muscular, energetic man in his mid forties. Perpetually optimistic and good-natured, he'd come to rely on me to get his clients safely up the mountain. As he approached the porch he tossed me a *mate* tea gourd and held up a thermos of hot water.

"Well," Carlos said. "At least you still have some reflexes, Eugenio. I was about to give you up for dead."

"I'm not ready for the vultures just yet," I said with a smile. "In fact I feel really good today."

"Good. I'm counting on it. We have a new client."

"Hold on a moment. I'll get the *mate*." I went inside my house and returned with a tin of tea leaves. After filling the gourd with the green herb, I inserted the metal straw and added hot water from the thermos.

"How many?" I asked.

"Two archeologists from Salta. I met them earlier today. They've been contracted by the archeological museum here in Cachi to survey the ruins in this area and look for artifacts to add to their collection. The director of the museum told them about the Incan ruins up on the peaks. They want us to take them up there so they can do some exploratory excavations. Can you make it?"

I handed the gourd of tea to Carlos. "Yes. I'll go. I suppose they'll need mules?"

"Yes, six mules to carry all their equipment to the high base camp. Pablo is coming. He'll provide the mules."

"How long will we be up there?"

"Seven days," Carlos replied, "but we'll carry supplies for twelve days in case they want to extend their stay. Given the clientele and what I was able to charge them, I'm paying twice the usual rate, which should come close to five thousand pesos to you — that is, if you can last that long. Can I count on you?"

"Of course you can, Carlitos. I haven't let you down yet."

"I suppose not. But you seem to be slowing down, and I sometimes worry you won't be able to keep up. Plus, I can't help thinking about our last trip, how disoriented and confused you became from the effects of the altitude. You know as well as I do that many climbers who get this way never make it back down."

"Yes, I remember. We climbed over fifteen hundred meters in one day. That's too much. We need to pace ourselves better so our bodies can adjust. Anyway, like I said, I feel good."

"Ok then. I'll pick you up tomorrow morning at six."

"I'll be ready."

We finished our tea and watched the shadows lengthen over the village streets where the children ran, shouting gleefully as one of them kicked a deflated soccer ball into a box crate goal.

* * *

Carlos picked me up early the next morning as promised and we drove to meet the archeologists at their hotel by the town plaza. The two men from Salta greeted us warmly and asked many questions related to the weather, the route, and the logistics of our expedition. One of them,

Santiago Madeo, was a tall, lanky fellow with a floppy military-style hat, wire-framed glasses, and a scraggly beard. His colleague, Ignacio Sarmiento, was short and stocky. He wore a dark gray wool hat with petroglyph designs and a green fleece jacket that looked too small for him.

We headed northwest, throwing clouds of dust behind us on a dirt road that skirted the river. On the side of the road, beneath the shade of a tree, we passed a crude shrine composed of stacks of water bottles and flowers, in honor of a woman named Difunta Correa, who, according to legend, got lost in the desert with her child and wandered for weeks looking for help. Gauchos found her dead not long afterwards, her small child clinging to her, suckling, miraculously, her "ever full" breast. Considered a saint by the people, her admirers built shrines along the road in her honor, leaving bottles of water as relief for the lost and thirsty.

After a short drive we entered the small pueblo called Las Pailas, where we met the arriero mule driver, Pablo Gonzalez. Las Pailas, a cluster of mud homes, was a singular exhibition of unlikeness — with lush, verdant irrigated fields contouring the flood plain, contrasting starkly with the eroded brown dirt-covered hills studded with cacti and scrub brush, punctuated by a backdrop of snow-capped peaks.

Pablo was an elderly yet vigorous man who lived alone with his wife in a one-room adobe hovel. Weathered by age and toil and the unforgiving harshness of the Puna sun, he had spent his entire life in Las Pailas, and knew every lomo and arroyo, every man, woman and child along with most of the animals that called this valley home. Extending a leathery hand, he introduced himself to the archeologists, and, after the usual exchange of pleasantries, consulted with Carlos on the disposition of the mules. "We are all are well fed and ready to march," he said, pointing with pride to his corralled animals. "Pachamama welcomes all travelers to her mountains, but only if they show her due respect."

The archeologists smiled at the appeal of the arriero, and nodded their agreement to the terms of travel presented by this citizen of the mountains.

As Pablo loaded the mules, Carlos gathered the archeologists around a crude wooden table beneath an alamo tree. He spread before them a topographical map of the area.

"El Nevado de Cachi is a complex of nine distinct peaks," he said. "Four of these peaks have some evidence of Incan ruins on their summits: Meléndez; La Pirámide, Di Pasquo, and San Miguel de Palermo. There are other Incan sanctuaries scattered across these mountains — many are still unexplored. But if I were you, I wouldn't get my hopes up. They are little more than piles of rock where they once performed rituals and ceremonies. You have the right to dig at these sites since you have a permit; but I want to emphasize the need to do so in a way that minimizes the impact to these mountains. This is a very fragile environment. El Nevado de Cachi doesn't get the sort of traffic that other high altitude peaks like Aconcagua get, but we're concerned nevertheless with protecting the integrity of the environment and limiting the influences of people whenever possible."

The taller of the two archeologists, Santiago, assured him they would remediate any excavated areas. "No one wants to scar this beautiful land, I promise you."

The other archeologist, Ignacio, agreed, and added, "We should also be careful to keep the locations of any finds as confidential as possible, at least until we gain full control of any promising sites."

Carlos nodded. "Las Pailas is itself a pre-Columbian site," he told them. "We could have a look around before we leave if you like."

"We'll pass for now," Santiago replied, "It's not that we aren't interested. It's just that we focus our research on sites located at four thousand meters elevation and above. We can have a look when we return."

"This expedition," Ignacio clarified, "is for the most part probative, meaning we don't anticipate any extensive digging. Our goal is simply to determine the best locations for more detailed follow up investigations. These things always take time. And the truth is, we are in no hurry."

I caught the surreptitious wink that Ignacio gave his partner after this last comment, and surmised, not without some cynicism, that the longer this project went on the more money they made. The archeological museum in Cachi was hardly a deep-pocket benefactor for these men; on the contrary, it was a small, locally run organization with significant scope in terms of protecting regional archeological sites, but with limited resources from the government.

With the mules now fully loaded, we shouldered our packs and followed a dirt track claimed by Pablo to be an old Incan road. I took up the rear. We walked in silence for several hours, passing out of the lower farmlands, beyond the fields of drying peppers — the bright, incongruously red patchwork on the hillsides — and into the dusty landscape of tall cactus, sand, and scrub brush. The weather was calm and cool, with few clouds in the sky. We passed in silence a line of vicuña — lithe, elegant creatures related to the llama but smaller in size, whose wool was once worn by Incan royalty.

By the end of the day we arrived at the Piedra Grande campsite, a barren location at 4,200 meters altitude, demarcated by a large, weathered boulder and covered with lichen-covered rock shards and tufts of dry grass.

We set up camp, pitching our tents near the landmark boulder to protect us from the wind. I prepared a thick stew called locro, a popular dish in the Andes made from corn, beef, pumpkin, and onions; and we passed the rest of the afternoon relaxing, drinking tea, and contemplating the enormous ridgeline of peaks that lay before us.

Pablo brought the *mate* gourd over to me and commented, in a harsh, gravelly voice, "You should know that Pachamama is not happy with us."

"What do you mean?" I asked, surprised by this statement. Though I had never openly professed a belief in the ancient deities, I had watched as a child the quiet whispers of my parents appealing to the gods for well-being, and had myself, from time to time, made my own silent prayers to these inscrutable gods. "How do you know this?"

"I've lived in these mountains all my life," Pablo said, rubbing his calloused knuckles gently across his woolen vest. "So has my family, as far back as any of us can remember. We've taken many travelers through these valleys and up to these peaks, always knowing that they are sacred places that shouldn't be trampled through and pillaged, like the old days when the Spaniards first came to Cachi. It feels like that now — that we are on a mission to pillage. She senses this too, and so does not look favorably on our being here."

I crossed my arms and looked away, unsure what to think of these superstitious proclamations.

"You feel it too," he said. "I can tell just by looking at you. There is a halo of sadness about you."

"You don't know what I feel, old man. Not even I know that."

The mule driver let out a soft grunting sound, and leveled his gaze at me. "I made an offering of llama before we left, like I usually do," he said. "But I knew just hours into this trip that this didn't satisfy Pachamama." He took from me the empty tea gourd and refilled it. "Just be careful. That's all I'm saying."

"The only thing that matters to me right now," I said, not without some impatience, "is that we get up the mountains and back in one piece so that we can get paid. Understand me?"

Pablo frowned and spat through his teeth onto his cracked knuckles. "Yes," he said. "I understand you perfectly."

* * *

We spent the next three days acclimatizing at the Piedra Grande base camp in preparation for higher elevation ascents. We made day hikes up to the lower peaks to gain altitude and accustom our bodies to the low oxygen environment, returning to camp to recuperate.

On the third day the archeologists searched the hills along the river for evidence of ceremonial sites, but returned to camp having found nothing. "We did find some interesting pottery shards," Ignacio said, extending his hand to show them a broken piece with a painted design that appeared to represent a storm cloud. "Pre-Incan Calchaquí, about six hundred years old. Nothing unusual really. This stuff can be found in a lot of places if one looks hard enough."

On the fourth day we packed up our gear and headed to our second campsite situated at the end of an expansive glacial valley called El Anfiteatro Kuhn. The glacier that had cut this valley had long ago melted, leaving behind a scattered moraine of rocks and boulders once carried inexorably downhill by a river of ice. Four of the El Nevado de Cachi peaks surrounded this high valley, its majestic scenery inspiring somberness and quiescence. After pitching our tents on a level spot of ground, we sat around the camp stove and watched as an enormous bank of white cloud slowly inched its way into the amphitheater from the valley below. "Magnificent," Carlos observed, sipping from his cup of coffee. "And at the same time, strangely terrifying."

Santiago agreed. "One feels so insignificant in a place like this. We spend our lives on trivialities, thinking everything we do is important and lasting. But none of it is. Even these mountains will one day be washed out to sea."

Pablo took out his bag of coca leaves — a common Andean antidote against altitude sickness — and passed it around. "Everything has its own significance," he said pensively. "No matter how small it is."

At that moment Ignacio, who lay on the ground with his back against a boulder, made a face as if suddenly struck by an unbearable pain, and cut loose a rumbling, sonorous fart. "Don Pablo," he said wryly, "can you interpret for me the significance of that noise?"

We laughed.

"I would guess," Carlos volunteered, "that it means our friend, Eugenio, put too much spice in the stew."

Over the course of the next five days, from our base camp in the glacial valley, we explored the summits and flanks of three peaks: Meléndez, Hoygaard, and San Miguel de Palermo. On the small crest of Palermo Peak, at an altitude of 6,000 meters, we found a semi-circular Incan structure, a few feet in height, formed of stacked granitic rocks. After digging in and around the structure for several hours without any luck, we abandoned the effort, and headed back to camp. "I was hopeful this structure might contain something," Ignacio later said. "But it appears to be a dry hole."

Carlos encouraged us to make a bid for the summit of El Libertador, the highest peak in the range at 6,380 meters, located north from the *cumbre* Hoygaard along a narrow ridgeline. "No one has found any ruins on El Libertador," he said, "but it would be a shame if we didn't have a crack at it while we're here." We agreed, and the following day Carlos, the two archeologists, and myself struck out to make a higher camp. From there we would make a final push to the summit. Pablo stayed behind with the mules, insisting he would be perfectly fine on his own.

We awoke the following morning and began our ascent as the sun broke over the range, throwing streaks of light across the rounded, snow-covered mountains like lighthouse beacons. After three hours of climbing we made the pass off the north end of Hoygaard Peak, and from there began the ridgeline hike to the apex of El Libertator. The ridge itself was composed of alternating patches of snow and loose scree exposed by strong winds. We found the trail easy to negotiate, but exercised caution, especially as the eastern slopes were heavily blanketed with snow and would spell disaster for us if we fell.

Upon reaching the summit we shook our fists and bellowed in exuberant triumph, slapping each other on the back and embracing each other like long lost brothers. We took several victory photos, and admired the incredible view that stretched before us for miles on end. The archeologists surveyed the summit for signs of Incan structures but, finding none, decided to turn back.

We had marched only a few hundred feet back down the ridge when something caught my eye as I glanced down the side of the mountain. It was a small ledge on the eastern slope, a flattened area partially covered with snow, easily accessible from the ridge, with what appeared to be a small mound of rock on it. The shape of the mound was not particularly conspicuous at first glance — there were several natural undulations in the rocky terrain which might easily have been overlooked; and yet, on closer inspection, I became convinced that this mound was not natural at all, that in fact it must have been shaped by human hands. I called to the others who were further down the ridge, shouting at them that I'd found something, to hurry back to my location so we could investigate. But my companions, tired and eager to return to lower camp, waved impatiently at me to follow them down the mountain. They turned away and kept walking.

I stepped carefully down onto the snowy slope, stabbing my ice ax firmly into the virgin snow. I knew this to be a foolish decision — I was alone, exhausted, and susceptible to imbalanced steps — yet something beckoned to me in this moment, urging me forward with ineffable whispers in spite of my inclination to quickly vacate this inhospitable place. Regaining a degree of confidence in my own sure-footedness, I kick-stepped my way down to the small ledge and found a small enclosure of rock, a shrine with an opening that faced the valley, situated such that its contents could not be seen from the summit.

Inside the enclosure there sat a tiny, hunched figure, its head resting downward and slightly to the left, as if sleeping. I fell forward onto my hands, staring at the dead child in the sarcophagus of rock, frozen in place — a mummified girl left to die of exposure, abandoned like the sacrificial Incan children found entombed on the high volcano, Llullaillaco. A dark brown woolen blanket lay wrapped around her shoulders, pinned by a gold clasp that had come loose, exposing a ceremonial dress adorned with blue and red beads. Her finely braided hair covered her sagging cheeks, blackened on one side as if burnt by lightning. Her hands lay in her lap, her death grip clutching a familiar figurine of clay.

I averted my eyes from this strange scene, and wondered if I was hallucinating from the effects of the altitude. Had it not happened on our last expedition? Had not Carlos found me stumbling and ranting on the way down from the summit of Meléndez? Did he not guide me down the mountain arm in arm as I shouted at the apparitions that followed us? Like then my movements were slow and labored as I struggled against an oppressive feeling of inertia; but I now knew with great clarity that I had full control of my senses. And when it came to me, so viscerally

— what it was that she held in her clutching hand — who I was, who I had been, and who I was yet to be — altered, in a moment cold and lifeless, irrevocably. For what the little girl held was the toy that I had made over twenty years ago, the llama that Amelia had always carried with her — the beloved toy that never left her grasp.

I closed my eyes and saw a procession of villagers carrying her up the mountain, full of resurrected beliefs and clandestine hopes that Pachamama would put an end to their lingering misfortunes. A deluge of oppressive, unanswerable questions began to surface — a chaotic fusion of rage, incomprehension, and claustrophobia. At its end came an ugly realization, an inescapable decision forcing me to choose how I would come to live with this ungodly reunion: believe that my daughter's death had not been in vain, that the forfeiture of her life had satiated the gods and released prosperity upon the people. Trust that her death had counted for something substantive in the movement of our lives. Or view it plainly for the abomination that it was — as an archetype of man's ignorance and depravity. Could I summon the courage to believe in the promise of sacrifice, to be as guilty as they of rejecting reason for the sake of hope? The uncertainty of it exhausted me, waning only in the realization that the second choice, the one of anger and retribution, meant spending the rest of my days consumed by nightmares and madness.

I buried my head in my hands and began to weep. A powerful desire to sleep overwhelmed me. I struggled to take in the thin mountain air, my lungs constricting within my chest, my heart pounding rapidly, defiantly. Outside of the enclosure, a mournful wind howled; large snowflakes whirled fitfully by. Perhaps the river would flood next year. The farmers could irrigate their crops. The animals would thrive and give milk. The wine would be plentiful, if only the snow would keep falling.

I reached out to Amelia with a quivering hand and gently caressed her cheek. Whispering my goodbyes, I wrapped my woolen scarf snugly around my neck, and cautiously made my way down the narrow ridge of El Nevado de Cachi.

II.
MEXICO

The Crater Of Orizaba

Harris took a seat on a stone bench in the plaza of Tlachichuca and scanned the dingy, whitewashed buildings that surrounded the square: the bakery, the church, the corner kiosk, the café where the old men congregated to discuss political events and the latest chismes. Several villagers, mostly of Tlascalan descent, were staring at him from the street corners. It was not unusual to see hikers tramping through the village in their heavy leather boots, especially in the winter months when the weather was more suitable for climbing.

A bank of mist rolled into the plaza from the southeast, advancing in protean formation down the slopes of the volcanic plateau. Harris felt light-headed. He retrieved his water bottle, took long, refreshing swigs, and threw his gaze eastward to study the massive volcanic cone that lorded over the village like an ancient Aztec pyramid. Situated in the Sierra Madre Oriental, and standing at over 18,400 feet in height, Orizaba was the third highest mountain in North America. Though not a technically difficult mountain, Harris knew that its steep, glaciated slopes commanded caution and respect from even the most experienced of climbers.

A young boy of about ten was standing by a flagpole nearby, listening to a radio and munching on a local confection. "*Oye, chico,*" Harris called to the boy. "*Estoy buscando la oficina de la Sociedad de Alpinismo. ¿Sabes dónde queda?*"

The boy pointed toward the church. "*Seis cuadras para allá,*" he said.

He made his way down a narrow street, sidestepping the dogs and scurrying children, and found himself in the midst of a bustling town market where throngs of people meandered through the gauntlet of vendors selling fruits, vegetables, poultry, textiles and pottery. A gray woolen cap hanging on a stand caught his eye and he paused to buy it from an old woman, who smiled at him and nodded repeatedly in gratitude. He donned the cap and continued on. Turning a corner, he at last found the office of the local Alpine club – a decrepit adobe structure with missing roof tiles and a broken window. Over the door hung a sign that read: Sociedad de Alpinismo.

"*Buenas tardes,*" he called to the man seated behind a desk at the back of the room. "*Soy Sidney Harris. Acabo de llegar de Puebla. ¿Es usted el Sr. Garza?*"

The man stood up, revealing a tall, lanky frame. "Hello," he said in English. He took off his reading glasses and smiled broadly, waving for Harris to come inside. "Julio Garza, at your service. Please come in, Sr. Harris. I've been expecting you."

Harris approached, the dusty wooden floor slats creaking loudly as he crossed the room. He was invited to take a seat on an old leather coach. Garza took the leather chair nearby. A simple wooden coffee table lay strewn with magazines and books on mountaineering. On the brick wall behind them, by the cast iron stove, hung a pair of crampons and an old ice axe.

Garza welcomed him graciously, serving coffee on a silver tea service, along with cookies that he claimed his sister had made for him. He appeared to be a man in his early forties: clean-shaven, his hair thin and slightly receding, his eyes dark green. Harris found his manner intelligent and cordial. He asked him jokingly if he'd been trained for diplomatic service.

"No. My profession is far less noble than diplomacy," Garza replied. "Years ago I lived in California, where I took a degree in Political Science from Stanford University. But now I am here — an underemployed lawyer in this little village — who spends most of his time engaged in his hobby. Running a guide service doesn't pay much, but I love the camaraderie and spirit of the climbing community." He stooped over and threw some kindling into the stove. "Perhaps," he said, pretending an air of confidence, "I am really just having what you Americans call the 'mid-life crisis'."

Harris laughed. "Thank God for that. We'd all become terrible bores without it. Must be a natural defense mechanism."

The guide looked Harris over, as if critiquing him. "You strike me as someone who is no stranger to a challenge."

"Very little in the way of Man-Against-Nature, I'm afraid."

"And where did you learn your Spanish?"

"In Barcelona. I worked there for two years."

"Ah, I could hear it in the accent, in the slight whistling emphasis on the 's' ... *buenas-s tardes-s.* You probably know that most of the young thrill-seekers who come here from the States speak very little Spanish. That is a real shame."

Harris sipped some of the stout Mexican coffee. "Yes, but I do envy their energy and enthusiasm."

"*Claro que sí,*" Garza conceded with a nod. "But it is often reckless, you know. I see people come to this area from all over the world, all of them so determined to reach the summit, as if their lives depended on it — you might even say, as if their lives would be meaningless without it."

"I'm sure that's part of the attraction," Harris said. "That simplicity of purpose. Just reach the top. Nothing more complicated than that."

"Well. It may be simple in concept. But in practice, it's highly complex."

"How do you mean?" Harris was impressed with Garza's strong command of English. His accent and articulation were flawless.

"I mean that mountaineering is highly unpredictable: one moment you are standing on a cliff looking out into the valley below. The next moment you are at the bottom of the cliff, coughing up blood. Summiting a high altitude peak is an achievement of endurance and will — its complexity lies in how we deal with the unexpected."

"In other words," Harris offered, "you never know what's going to happen next."

"Exactly. And because you never know, when the moment comes and you are forced to draw from whatever resources you have left, you sometimes discover hidden attributes about yourself — things that lay dormant. Put another way, an expedition may reveal to you and to your companions that when push comes to shove you are an untrustworthy shit. I've seen this happen more than once. Some inevitably run off ahead of everyone else — they can't wait to be the first one to the top — and they leave their companions far behind, maybe to die in a crevasse or an avalanche. On the other hand, I've also seen some wondrous acts of courage and selflessness. I once saw a man on a climb in Bolivia give up his sleeping bag to his friend, whose goose down bag had dislodged from his pack and was nowhere to be found. It was minus 40 degrees when the sun set, and yet this man — Miguel was his name — gave up his bag to his friend, who was suffering from altitude sickness. The sick one lived through the night, but we found Miguel dead the next morning."

Harris stared for a moment at the lawyer. He knew that Garza was sizing him up, testing him with worst-case scenarios, probably all of them true. Understandable, given his line of business.

"Whatever their motivations," Garza continued, "many who come to Tlachichuca seem to be attuned to this complexity, or at least have spent some time anticipating it, meaning they have some comprehension of what they are up against. Others have no clue whatsoever; they come here ill prepared, having no firm understanding of the element of risk. They just want to say: 'I climbed a high volcano in

Mexico,' but I doubt very much they experience any personal growth or unearth any meaningful insights. There were a few in here like that last week — a group of three young men from Japan. They had never climbed a mountain before; but they struck out on their own four days ago, making a bid for the summit from the Piedra Grande base camp. There was a big snow up on the mountain after they left. No one has heard from them since."

The stove let go of a loud crack. Garza took a climbing pole from against the wall and closed the stove door with the end of it. "Did you know," he said, "that Cortez and his men once came through this area?"

"Yes. I had heard that."

"The conquistadors were no different than we are today. They wanted to explore the mountain and see first hand what mysteries it concealed. At that time it was blowing a lot of steam and ash into the air, and they had never seen anything like it before. Some claim that two of his soldiers made it to the top, but others are not so sure."

"Is that the climber's journal we spoke about over the phone?" Harris pointed to a large, hardbound book on the coffee table.

"Yes," Garza said, somberly. "You will find what you are looking for in that book."

Harris took up the journal, entitled "*Apuntes de Viaje,*" and opened it to the page marked by a slender red ribbon. He scanned the entries, many of them smudged and hastily written, others carefully thought out and exceptionally well drafted. He found the trip report from William J. Foster of Seattle, Washington, USA, dated February 3, 2005. It ran as follows:

We stayed two nights at the Octavio Alvarez base camp hut at 14,000 feet. John and I both felt surprisingly well, though several other climbers in the camp were clearly in bad shape from the altitude. One climber from Oregon lay moaning all day in his sleeping bag, wheezing with every breath and throwing up every time he tried to eat something. His guide took him out the next day.

We hit the trail at 4 am, 1/31, and meandered our way, our headlamps illuminating the path ahead of us, through the rocky gully. To our great surprise, we found several crosses planted in the moraine alongside the trail and on the top of the cliffs, evidently remembrances of the many fallen climbers from decades past. It was ominous. We felt as though we were walking through a graveyard. Images of the dead climbers, like caricatures in the Mexican Day of the Dead festivals, floated through my mind. We spoke little during this initial phase of the climb, but redoubled our determination to make the summit safely and return before dusk.

At the end of four hours we reached the bottom of the Jamapa Glacier, at roughly 16,000 feet. By then the weather had completely cleared — the sun was shining brightly and our faces quickly burned in the high altitude UV light. We found that our strength quickly dissipated at this height; every movement we made took enormous effort, and we realized there was no room for mistakes on the slippery traverse that lay ahead of us. We roped up. I took the lead. We kick-stepped our way up the snow-covered slope, slowly and deliberately, and it seemed that the more we rested the more tired we grew, so we slogged onward with no rest stops, just slow, methodical steps, inching our way up the mountain in measured increments. The higher we got the more incredible the view became — we could see for miles in every direction, and we had a very clear view of the other snow-capped volcano to the West: Popocatépetl.

A few hours later, exhausted and dehydrated, we found ourselves standing on the crater's edge. It was an incredible view. Unbelievably exhilarating. The snow-filled crater was blackened from the sporadic venting of gas, and fell sharply before us several hundred feet. We wondered if the Indians had tossed human sacrifices into this volcanic orifice, if some had simply fallen in and not been able to climb back out. We made jokes, like: "I've fallen and I can't get out," and slapped each other on the back in congratulations of such an amazing feat. We were punchy from the lack of oxygen — from the adrenaline rush of being in such a magnificent place. I'm incapable of describing adequately what we felt at that moment. How does one articulate what is intrinsically indefinable? Perhaps it is this very wordless quality itself that is the ultimate prize.

We saw a climber far below us, a speck at the base of the cone where the snowline began, wandering about like a wind up toy. We recognized immediately that he was in trouble, and so we decided to head back down. We did not rope up this time — why I don't know. Possibly we were not thinking clearly, or were simply anxious to get off the mountain. At the very least, we were not as careful as we had been on the way up.

I don't remember seeing the moment John fell, but I remember hearing him hit the snow and the sound of his jacket scraping the snow as he slid down the slope head over heels. I cried out to him. He did not make a sound — never once cried out. His ice ax was still strapped to his wrist and I could see that he was frantically attempting to secure it with both hands in order to make an attempt at self-arrest. But it was futile. The speed of his descent would not allow him to gain the control he needed to correctly position his body and ice ax. So he fell. He fell for over a thousand feet down the steep slopes of Orizaba, and when I reached him I found him still alive, but only semi-conscious. His face was bloodied from the ice scraping against his flesh. Both of his legs were broken. I did not know it at the time but the end of his ice ax had stabbed into his chest and punctured one of his lungs. There was blood coming out his ears, and also from his mouth as he attempted to speak to me. I was alone then. There was no one around who could help us — even the climber in trouble was no longer to be seen. I knew I was in no condition to carry him out, that he would die if I attempted it. So I waited for help to arrive. John struggled to hold on. I covered him in my jacket and cradled him in my arms to keep him warm. I talked to him, and I believe he could understand what I said. We waited for over an hour before anyone came, but by then it was too late. In one of his last moments of lucidity he expressed his assurances that, in spite of what had just happened, he had no regrets. At the time I did not believe him, but I see now that he was simply coming to terms with his own decision to make the climb. John had risked his life to reach the summit. To express remorse for having taken that risk when triumph had been so beautifully realized would, for him, be an act of dishonor.

Harris closed the book and looked away, clearly unnerved by what he had just read. Garza folded his hands together and watched Harris closely, but said nothing. For several minutes they sat in silence, interrupted only by the crackles of the fire.

Finally, Harris said: "After reading this, I can appreciate what you said earlier — about how stress can reveal hidden aspects of character."

Garza gave him a puzzled look. "Oh? How so? I found nothing in the report that indicated Foster acted inappropriately."

"No, it's not in the report," Harris replied. "It's in the story that he told afterwards. When Foster returned to Seattle he told us point blank that he and John had been roped together on their descent. This report exposes that story as a lie." He looked now at Garza, betraying a hint of mistrust, as though he now suspected that the guide had in some way conspired with Foster's fabrication. "I suppose he thought none of the family would ever come down here to visit this place, much less find this journal."

"You do realize," Garza cautioned, "that if they had been roped together, John might have pulled them both down the mountain. They might have both lost their lives."

Harris scoffed. "You know as well as I do that he might also have stopped his fall. And besides, that's no excuse for what he did."

"No, of course not. Foster's lie is inexcusable. But he has no liability in this matter. Things often go wrong on the mountain, no matter how carefully we prepare. In any event, I'm very sorry about what happened—" He reached for the coffee and, with a quietly spoken "*con permiso*", poured more coffee into Harris's cup.

"So then. Are we still on for tomorrow? There is a cross marking the spot where John died. I can take you there once you've acclimated."

"Yes. I want to see the marker, but I also want you to guide me to the summit. I want to know what he saw up there that made him so dammed glad that he did it."

Garza looked pensively at the American. "Very well," he said. "I'll take you to the crater of Orizaba. But I can't guarantee you will experience what your brother John did — not everyone has that privilege. To some, the trek up Orizaba is a pilgrimage, a quest to find the stuff we are made of. To others, Orizaba is just another peak to be bagged. If I were you I would consider carefully your reasons for attempting the summit. As I said before, you may discover things about yourself that you may later wish you had left dormant."

Harris sipped the remainder of his coffee and stood up to go. "You seem to have the instincts of a good lawyer," he said with a quick smile. "I hope your instincts as a guide are equally sharp."

Garza leaned back in his chair. "I hope you will do me one favor, Sr. Harris."

"Name it."

"While we're up there on the mountain," Garza now motioned to the window, to a perfectly framed view of the sunlit peak, whose apex stood cloaked with a dark lenticular cloud, "please keep a look out for those three Japanese climbers that I told you about. They might have family who care about them too."

III.
ASIA

Jameson's Letters

Jameson's letter came to me thirty days after its postmarked date, stamped with the face of a dour-looking Nepalese ruler. Within its tattered envelope I found shreds of wrinkled rice paper, scribbled with the indecipherable yet undeniable handwriting of my friend and climbing companion.

I envisioned Henry huddled in his tent, tucked into the crags of Everest, his headlamp illuminating his quivering writing paper, blowing into his blackened, frostbitten hands as he gathered his thoughts to tell me what he then had on his oxygen-deprived mind. His letter appeared to have once been crumbled into a ball, as if he'd given up in frustration and had tossed it away, only to reconsider and iron it out as best he could. Exhaustion must have weighed on him, his vision blurred from the onset of snow blindness. In spite of this, he renewed his effort, striking through words, cursing in whispers, giving up again, and finally ripping the sheet into small pieces and stuffing his scrambled thoughts into an envelope with a laugh.

From the day I announced that I was hanging up my crampons and no longer accompanying him on his increasingly risky climbs, Henry never forgave me for abandoning him, for dissolving what had been a solid partnership — I, his trusted Sancho Panza, loyally following him on his journeys of peril and absurdity.

His letters came to me from all over the world, randomly, unexpectedly. On one occasion he sent me a small package from Africa following his descent from Kilimanjaro. It contained a large ball of dung formed by the endless rolling of that famous beetle.

"This is my friend, Matt," said the note that came with it. "A well-rounded individual, to be sure; but in the end, still a turd."

A year later I received a letter from China that contained nothing more than a page torn from a Beijing newspaper. He had circled a cluster of characters and scrawled into the margin: "They're at it again." Neither of us understood a word of Chinese. But to Henry, that was precisely the point.

Forever spotlighting the inscrutable, Henry religiously believed that exploring the unknown was our highest calling. We had experienced much together on our travels, helping each other down from high altitude peaks and marveling near death at the unexpected lengths of our own limits. We'd nursed each other back to health from infectious diseases, lacerations and broken bones; gotten drunk on the local spirits; bailed each other out from foreign jails; and, when the gods smiled down on us, slept with the local women. He thrived on this camaraderie, his spirit quickly dissipated by anything that smacked of inertia or complacency. It was not thrill-seeking that motivated him. No. Whatever wanton demon it might be named, it drove him to the ends of the earth with an ever-increasing obsession. He wanted desperately for me to rejoin him on his quests to explore what he cryptically referred to as "The Tangent," and though tempted by this siren call, I knew I could no longer go on with it. The money wasn't there anymore. The seasoning that age brings opened my eyes to my own mortality. Pragmatic concerns now dominated my thoughts: The need for higher education. The struggle to make a living. The desire to find a woman, win her affection, make a home, raise a family. The usual stuff of life, all of which now stood between Henry and me. And, of course, he would not abide any of it.

"Dear Infidel," he once wrote me from Karachi. "Abandon your false gods. Save your withering soul. Come to Pakistan and climb Nanga Parbat with me." And that was the last I'd heard from him.

* * *

I poured the bits and pieces of Jameson's letter onto my writing desk and arranged each shred flat, ink side up, in the right order. "Meet me at the Hotel Florid Nepal in Kathmandu," it read. "I found Mallory's camera."

Henry's latest ploy to lure me out of the suburbs brought a smile to my face. "The Tangent" in this case was a mystery that dates back to June of 1924, when George Mallory, the English mountaineer who famously retorted "Because it's there" to the question of why attempt Everest, made the tragic first attempt. He and his climbing companion, Sandy Irvine, were last seen on the Second Step of the Northeast ridge, a few hours below the summit. A cloud of mist enveloped them, and they were never seen again.

Mallory's bleached white body, well-preserved in the anoxic environment, was found in 1999, lying face down in the snow and scree at 8,160 meters altitude. His pockets contained various artifacts: a folding knife, altimeter, goggles, bits of twine; but nowhere to be found was the Vest Pocket Kodak camera that was known to have been carried on the climb. Neither was found the photo of Mallory's wife, which Mallory claimed he would place on Everest's summit, leading many to believe that since it wasn't on his corpse he likely made it to the top after all. If indeed he had made it to the top, then surely he had taken a picture with his Kodak. So the theory went. But the expeditions launched to find and retrieve the cameras of Mallory and Irvine had been in vain.

* * *

For days I tried to shrug it off, but the astonishing declaration in Jameson's letter was impossible to ignore. It haunted my thoughts, distracted me into states of forgetfulness, and drove impatience in my replies to those around me. Why this letter, out of all the letters he'd sent littered with outlandish statements, had so knocked me off balance, I can only attribute to the inescapable possibility *that it might actually be true.*

Much to the chagrin of my friends and family, whose concerned looks clearly indicated a loss of faith in me, I flew to Kathmandu and inquired for my friend at the hotel desk. It was a hostel, actually. Frugal. Sparsely furnished. Adorned with faded posters of Annapurna and Everest. The rooms were less than three Euros a night, which attracted many of the poor wayward youths of the world who shared Henry's wanderlust. Climbers constantly came and went from this place, some crackling with a familiar electricity of anticipation, others carrying their sunburns and climbing injuries like badges of honor.

The face of the little man who ran the place lit up when I mentioned Henry's name. "Yes, I know him," he said, in a harried tone. "But I have not seen him in two weeks, so I had to rent his room to someone else. He owes me one week room charges."

A group of young climbers sitting on a bench against the wall suddenly grew quiet.

One of them, a red-headed, lanky twenty-something dressed in a black North Face jacket, approached me.

"Are you a friend of Henry Jameson?" he asked.

"Yes," I answered. "Do you know him?"

"I knew him," he said. "He was our guide."

He introduced himself as Steven Walcott and asked if I was Matt Sawyer.

"Yes. How did you know my name?"

"Henry told us you might be coming. He talked a lot about the trips you guys made together."

"You said you knew him. Have you seen him recently? He wrote me that he was here in Kathmandu, staying at this hostel."

"I'm sorry to have to tell you this," the young man said. "But Henry died on Everest five days ago from cerebral edema. We found him staggering outside his tent at Camp 3, rambling incoherently about a camera that he'd found recently on the Tibetan route. Believe me, we did everything possible to stabilize him so that we could take him down. We gave him dexamethasone and put him in a hyperbaric bag, but he was too far gone and couldn't be moved. He died that same morning as the sun came up."

A few of the other young climbers had gathered around us. Some of them gripped me by the shoulder and expressed their sorrow, lamenting how losing a good friend is one of the worst of all pains in life, that they had also lost good friends to the mountain, and though they had not known Henry for very long, they liked him immensely and were very saddened by his loss.

They informed me that his body still lay on the mountain, covered with rock cairn, marked with his ice ax as a make-shift cross. Steven wrote down the coordinates for me, which he had taken on his GPS, in case I wished to visit him. "None of us knew if he had any family," he said. "You were the only one he ever spoke about."

"We have his gear with us," a tall Danish-looking girl told me, her English heavily accented. "We weren't exactly sure what to do with it. But I think if anyone should have it, it should be you."

She brought me his pack and a nylon carry bag. I thanked them for their kindness. They shook my hand vigorously, and some of them said goodbye with sympathetic hugs, displaying all the camaraderie that Henry had relished, the bond among climbers that he'd wanted to reconnect between us. I would never again feel that tie with him. But I took solace in the fact that he died doing that which he loved best.

* * *

On my return home I found it difficult to go through the motions. Work. Eat. Sleep. Worry about job security. Stress over financial volatility. Battle with insurance companies. Saving for college. Saving for retirement. The struggle against entropy, the inexorable deterioration of all things ... All this now dominated my thoughts. And while immersion in good books, time with family, dinner with friends, laughing at stupid jokes, made up for the nagging sense of loss, I still could not shake the desire to strike out into the unknown, into "The Tangent" that had seized the imagination of my friend Henry and men like him. Men like Hillary, Mallory, and Irvine.

Naturally, Mallory's camera was nowhere to be found. I looked for it in all the pockets of Henry's gear, but there was no Vest Pocket Kodak. What had become of it, whether it had really been found or was simply a delusional fantasy of Henry's, would never be known. But I did discover one camera — a digital camera that belonged to Henry. On its storage card I found a photo of Henry standing on the top of Everest with a big shit-eating grin on his face. There were other photos too, including one of us together on the top of Aconcagua, a peak in Argentina we'd climbed in February of 2004. The photo sits on my desk as a reminder of what we had once accomplished.

A month or so after my return, in preparation for a summer camping trip to Colorado, I pulled out Henry's backpack again to look for a First Aid kit I'd seen amongst his belongings. As I pillaged through the pockets, pulling out sundry gear and piling it onto the floor, a crumpled pad of paper, bundled in one of his shirts, spilled out onto the mound of equipment. I flipped through its pages, full of scribbles, doodles, drawings, and bursts of cosmic wisdom, and found, at the end of the pad, a letter addressed to me.

"I'm back at Everest Base Camp," it read. "On the Southeast Ridge this time, doing some guide work to earn some money so I can travel on foot to Llasa, like Heinrich Harrer described in *Seven Years in Tibet*. I have Mallory's camera with me. I have sewn it into my jacket so it will not be lost again. What do you bet it will have pictures of Mallory's naked wife on it? By the way, what's keeping you? Come to Llasa with me! Shangri La is real but it's no fun going it alone. Your friend, Henry."

I promised myself then that I would go back to Nepal, that I would locate my friend's grave with the coordinates Steven had given me and put to rest once and for all whether Mallory's camera had been found. But no, it will never come to pass. The drive is gone. My will is shot. I cannot look at my friend Henry frozen in death, the way they found Mallory. Let them both lie buried on the mountain where they belong.

Bay of Bengal

I had been telling stories at a bar in New Orleans — stories about finding oil through unorthodox means. "Not with dowsing rods," I said. "It's just a feeling that I get when I'm in the right spot." The cadre of patrons, many of whom worked in the petroleum industry as land men or roughnecks, laughed at my boasts, and paid for my drinks as tribute for the entertainment.

There was one among them, though, a rough looking sort with two missing fingers sheared off from the swinging of drill pipe, who did not scoff like the others. He smiled knowingly, and said that he recognized my name, having heard of it from a colleague who had sworn to him that he had followed my career and had come to believe that I did indeed possess an uncanny ability to find oil. "They say you've never had a dry hole," he announced, holding his glass up in honor of my reputation, "but whether this is from luck or a higher power, it's not for me to say."

Hearing this, an elderly gentlemen sitting next to me, an old oilman man named Albert Sand, said: "We used to see guys like you in the early days: black box peddlers in their funny suits and bowties — convicts mostly, midgets and fortune tellers, mind readers and travelling yogis with "Doctor" in their titles — always challenging us to test our luck for a finder's fee. We were so fascinated with these fellows that we even contracted one of them on a whim. One day we took him out into the swamps on a scouting mission. He got separated from us somehow. We searched for days for this man, but we never heard from him again."

This elderly gentlemen — rich beyond belief from his many discoveries and buoyed with life from the thrill of the hunt — laughed heartily, and, taking me by the arm as he walked me out of the bar, told me he would like to take me up on my offer, admitting that he did not believe in my pretensions but was extending me the courtesy irrespective of his disbelief out of a sportsman like feeling and frank admission that he longed for the days when fools had their respected place in the affairs of men. He invited me to join his company fishing expedition on his private yacht, and one hot day in June we motored a hundred miles offshore in the Gulf of Mexico to fish. On our return, roughly sixty miles out, the unmistakable current ran down my spine with a twinge that feels neither pleasant nor painful. I advised Sand to mark this spot and drill a well to a depth of fourteen thousand feet. "How do you know? How can you tell?" he kept asking me, annoyed and at the same time incapable of governing his excitement. As there was no rational answer I could provide him, he accepted my advice on faith, and the following week he instructed his staff to prepare studies and maps of the location using remote sensing data, which, as it turned out, presented a strong case for a subsurface trap. The prospect now legitimatized through scientific means, Sand set in motion the gears that turn in the hunt for oil. He spent ten million dollars in acquiring the lease and drilling the well. And it came in big, more than doubling his wealth when he later sold his interest in the newly discovered field. He would later joke about my "hunch", but would never openly admit that I was responsible for his discovery, instead chalking it up to the efforts of his staff. His reluctance to acknowledge my contribution changed, however: one night he came knocking on my door, swaying before me in a drunken stupor, waving in my face a check in the amount of fifty thousand dollars. He pressed me to form a partnership with him. I refused him on the grounds that I could never actually predict when the sense would come over me, or that it would ever come again, and that I would rather not be locked down with a partnership that might preclude other possibilities. The larger opportunities, I told him, lay abroad — in distant, virgin lands.

That opportunity came six months later when the head of the Burmese national oil company got a lead on me from Sand, who had been trying to broker an offshore deal with the South Koreans. As it turned out, the South Koreans had a working relationship with the Burmese in the Bay of Bengal. Sand had vouched for me. He swore by my "infallible sense", and soon afterwards, through a representative of the South Korean firm, I was presented with an offer to act as an exploration consultant for the Bay of Bengal project.

It is no exaggeration to say that Burma is one of the poorest and most backward countries in Southeast Asia, having a poorly educated populace and a severely degraded infrastructure. Its southern coast lay ravaged by a deadly cyclone. The country is owned and operated by a military junta whose main accomplishments include bankrupting the nation, plaguing it with human rights violations, and securing its place as a pariah in the eyes of the civilized world. For years the Burmese and their neighbor to the west, Bangladesh, had laid claim to offshore tracts in the Bay of Bengal, a lingering dispute that, on top of the anxiety of dealing with a repressive military regime, frightened away most Westerners.

Arriving in Burma on a hot summer day, I was whisked away in a limousine to a private compound in the center of Rangoon. The grounds were expansive — acres of cleanly shaved lawns; a large pond banked with flowering lotus; a dock with two rowboats; giant palm trees; paths that wound through tropical gardens; and an aviary with rare birds plucked from the depths of the amorphous jungle. In the center of it all lay a two-story house built in French colonial style. A contingent of household attendants, including men with Longyi garments draped around their waists, lived in small cabanas situated within the walled compound. My military escort, a small man with a pock-marked face, made it clear to the staff that I was a special guest of the state oil company, and that whatever I called for they would provide it to me without hesitation.

As I settled into my room, I heard a knock on the door. A slender woman dressed in a white blouse and a long blue skirt entered the room. She wore her hair in a bun but was otherwise bereft of feminine accents. She told me her name was Moon Mya Kyi, and inquired if my accommodations were comfortable. "I work for Myanma," she said pleasantly. "I will be your liaison while you're here."

The woman proceeded to explain to me the exploration program for the Bay of Bengal, and what my role in it would be.

"We will take you to areas offshore considered prospective. You will pinpoint for us which of these areas has the highest potential for large oil and gas deposits. Myanmar, or Burma as you call it, has limited financial resources. Your ability to locate economic oil deposits is critical to our success."

"We haven't finalized the terms of my contract yet," I said.

"Yes. I'm aware of that," the woman returned, nodding.

"If there's oil out there, offshore, I'll find it."

"There are many of us who sincerely doubt that, Mr. Langstrom. But it appears that some of our leaders, especially those from the interior regions where old superstitions are still popular, seem to think that people like you actually have the power to predict the unknown."

"And you don't believe this."

"No. I don't. I'm sorry."

"Then you probably consider my being here a waste of time and money," I observed, curious to know more about where she stood.

The woman held herself upright in her chair, her hands folded in her lap. "That is not for me to say," she said deferentially. "But if I were in your shoes, if I truly believed that I had such an ability, I would keep it to myself. I would allow my successes to be seen as a result of hard work and the application of principles and logic. Your decision to divulge this intuition of yours — to do so openly rather than be discreet about it — is a sign to many that you are not to be trusted."

"But hiding it would be dishonest, wouldn't it?" I asked, though I was careful not to display any defensiveness in my question.

"I merely suggest that discretion has its advantages."

"I've never once been wrong in my predictions," I said boldly. "Whether this is due to luck or a higher sense is unimportant. In the end, results are all that matter."

"Fortune tellers also say they are never wrong in their predictions," she pointedly observed, albeit in a disarming way.

I quietly admired this woman's poise, not to mention her strong command of English. I could find nothing to say in reply, which embarrassed me. I dropped a spoonful of sugar in my tea, and looked up at her to see what else she might say.

"What is it that you want, Mr. Langstrom?" she asked.

I hesitated before answering. "I'm willing to forego my fee for the location work, but in return I want a royalty interest in anything drilled."

She shook her head. "I'm sorry," she replied. "That might be a common arrangement in your country, but we cannot agree to this. If that condition is a showstopper for you, I understand; and we can go our separate ways."

"I'm afraid," I said as politely as possible, "that for me this would be a showstopper."

She drank some tea and asked if I would care for another cup, which I thanked her for.

"It could be years before we ever drill," she said. "And longer still to bring any oil we find to market."

"Yes. I'm aware of that."

We were quiet for a moment. Finally, she said, "I will ask about your royalty interest, and will let you know tomorrow if there is any flexibility on this demand."

"Thank you."

She smiled, and got up to leave.

"Mahatma Gandhi once said that Earth provides enough to satisfy every man's need, but not every man's greed," she said. "I hope you enjoy the rest of your day, Mr. Langstrom. Good afternoon. And please, call me Moon."

* * *

The following day a van with two armed soldiers, two civilians dressed in casual clothes, and Moon, arrived at the front of the house. The soldiers glared at me coolly behind their shades as they exited the vehicle and stood beside the van with their AK47's at the ready. One of the civilians, a middle-aged man with a pot-belly, noticed my hesitation and approached me with an extended hand. He introduced himself as the head of the exploration department at Myanma Oil and Gas. The other civilian, a South Korean, nodded and shook hands, smiling as if he were genuinely glad to see me.

I was told by the pot-bellied man that before any contracts could be signed my divining skills would be put to the test. If I passed the test my contract would include the royalty interest that I had requested. If I failed, I would immediately be taken in for questioning, and pressed to confess my plans to defraud the government of Myanmar. "Our national security forces are very good at extracting confessions," he told me with an ugly smile.

The world went dark as a black hood was placed over my head and cinched at my neck. I was led to the back seat of the van and seated between two men. As we drove off, the Burmese man said: "We will take you to twenty different locations where wells have already been drilled. At each of these spots we will exit the vehicle and you will have five minutes to determine if the location is capable of producing hydrocarbons. We, of course, already know the answer to that question. For you to pass this test you must be one hundred percent correct. No exceptions."

"I don't agree to this test," I objected behind my hood. "I can't always predict when the sense will come over me. I thought that was plainly disclosed to you."

Moon said something in Burmese to the others, and three of them, including the Korean, conversed for a few moments.

"No," she finally said. "We don't recall hearing that before. And if that is the case, then you might not be of much use to us."

"I'll need more than five minutes at each location," I said, angling for time.

"Not possible," the Burmese man said.

"Do you want to quit now?" Moon asked. "If you wish to quit, we can turn around and you can go back to the U.S. But once you agree to perform this test, there is no turning back."

I continued to argue for more time, as well as the option to back out before all the stops had been visited. They refused, and asked me rather curtly to make up my mind.

I was pondering my reply when the Korean, who was seated to the right of me, nudged me once, gently but firmly, with his elbow, and very faintly whispered: "Yes".

Before I could consider what he meant by this gesture, I felt two more nudges in rapid succession, after which followed an almost inaudible "No". It appeared he was attempting to establish a code of communication between us, though at the moment I failed to understand his motivation for doing so.

"Well? What's your decision?" the Burmese man asked.

I felt one nudge.

"Very well," I relented. "I agree to the test."

"Good," said the man. He uttered something in Burmese, and one of the soldiers sitting to the left of me uncinched my hood and inserted plugs into my nostrils and ears. He then replaced the hood.

We drove along a bumpy, potholed road in silence. After a long drive we approached our first stop. As the van slowed to a halt, I felt two quick nudges from the Korean.

The door slid open. I was led out of the van and let loose to meander about, hooded, unable to hear or smell, cautiously stepping on spongy ground, waiting to see if the finder sense would arise within the allotted time. In spite of my attempts to relax and be as receptive as possible, the feeling never came. Not even a hint. There was nothing left to do but to cling to dim hopes that I could rely on my own resources rather than the uncertain signals of a stranger that I had only just met.

At the end of five minutes, with little recourse left, I informed them that the location was dry.

This routine was repeated another nineteen times for the rest of the day. Not once did the finder sense arise during our stops, and thus all of my decisions were based on the telegraphed signals of the silent Korean. Of these, only two out of twenty were called as positive for hydrocarbons.

After the last site had been visited, I was returned to the compound, where I took a shower and ate a small plate of fish and rice noodles served to me by a quiet woman with shark-like eyes. A bottle of locally produced Dornfelder wine was opened, and I soon fell asleep, immersed in dreams of pythons crawling into my bed and suffocating me.

For the next two days I lay in my room watching the ceiling fan revolve in slow, off-kilter gyrations. It rained incessantly, at times ferociously. Gulliver's Travels lay on my nightstand. I read it with an odd mixture of pleasure and apprehension, wondering what judgments lay in store for me. An old RCA television kept me company. I watched it in vain attempts to tune my ear to the language, imagining conversations from the gestures and vocal intonations of the characters on the screen. I had no visits from Moon or the others, though the man with the pock-marked face could be seen strolling outside my room on the veranda, stealing glances at me as he walked by, and spitting betel nut juice into the potted planters.

My appetite quickly diminished; the food brought to me from the kitchen tasted greasy and bland. The woman who attended me refused to be lured into pantomime discussions, so I bided my time meditating on my future prospects, wondering whether I had been hung out to dry by the mysterious Korean.

On the third day my lassitude came abruptly to an end. I was lying in bed as usual, mindlessly watching television: a news program displayed scenes of the disastrous flood that had ripped through the Irrawaddy delta four months before my arrival. There was a story about a local soccer match; a story about farmers gaining access to electricity; and then the story of a foreigner branded a spy by the junta and sentenced to die. Shockingly, the execution of the accused played out live on the static-filled screen. The man, haggard and bruised, was stood against a wall. A black hood was placed over his head — a hood exactly like the one placed over my own head only days before — and with a sharp command and a volley of bullets, he was visited by finality. As his lifeless body slumped to the ground, a television commercial cut in for a popular breath mint, followed by footage of police quelling a riot of disaffected students in Mandalay.

The absurdity of the situation sent me into a panic. I'd had enough. It was time to go. I packed as much as I could carry in a small rucksack and lit out into the pouring rain, jumping over the compound wall and scuttling like a crab down a garbage-strewn alley. I wandered the wet streets of Rangoon, passing the golden spires of the Shwedagon pagoda and finding shelter in an abandoned rickshaw parked beneath the awning of a tenement building. The rain had stopped by then, and I managed to sleep a few hours before being awakened in the early morning light by a saffron-robed monk. He looked down on me with a curious expression, and peppered me with Burmese warnings interspersed with random English words. He extended his alms bowl. I promised him a 5,000 kyat note, which I had taken from my pocket and now waved before his face, if he could tell me where I could find the U.S. embassy. It took several tries before he understood me, but in the end the kyat bill successfully cut through the language barrier. With nods of assurance and a wily smile he accepted my offering and, taking me by the arm, guided me through the throngs of honking buses and trucks to the doorstep of my countrymen, whose flag flapped graciously in the wind like a signpost of salvation. They treated me strangely at first, as if they were unsure whether to help me or to turn me back out into the street. My appearance no doubt alarmed them. They wanted to know what kind of trouble I was in. I told them that I was not sure, that I had made a deal with the government and now believed it to be a deal with the devil, and that I needed to flee the country as quickly as possible. Though I lacked sufficient money to fully cover the expense, they kindly secured me passage on a merchant ship bound for Sydney. With the travel arrangements made, they shook my hand with firm, sympathetic grips, their eyes locking on my own with a mixture of pity and incomprehension. I thanked them for their generosity, and wished them all good fortune and a long and healthy life —

an ironic farewell that amused them, coming as it did from a compatriot in such dire straits.

It was a hundred miles out into the Bay of Bengal when I was gripped by the peculiar twinge that signals like a siren call the dark substance that we obsess over with such ravenous appetite. It smashed over me like a tidal wave; and I knew that a behemoth lay beneath me, colossal in dimension, larger than I'd ever sensed before or would ever sense again — miles below in the black subsurface depths — the strike of a lifetime that every diviner dreams of but never finds. And as I stood on the deck of the merchant vessel, nauseous and aware of the scavenger gulls swooping low in search of scraps, a new decision faced me. Should I turn back now and declare victory to Moon and the Burmese man? Should I tell them that I had accomplished my objective, that I had located untold wealth ensconced beneath their waves? Dare I demand my share of this wealth? No. I knew it was not to be. The risk was too great; the trust too little. The time had come to ignore the upwellings that would only carry me to my perdition. I resolved to set a new course: henceforth I would abandon the playbook of the augur, in search of a more stable life. Such was my state of mind as the ship pitched into the waves, heading south across the Bay of Bengal.

The Water Wheel (A Parable)

Many years ago, in a northern province of China, in a village called "Water Wheel", there lived an aspiring young artist named Yang Tzu who, since a very early age, possessed an extraordinary ability to paint the world around him in astounding, near-photographic detail. His parents, wealthy landowners not unfamiliar with the subtleties of the arts, were, nevertheless, members of a more pragmatic philosophy. Often they would shake their heads at their wistful son, and with great impatience say: "Yang Tzu, these are perilous times. You are eighteen years old now. It's time you give up your frivolous pursuits, learn some responsibility, and do some work around here. The Communists have already taken over the Huan estate. And just look what happened! It's terrible, just terrible! We think it's time we join together as a family. Otherwise we'll be next! They'll come, you'll see, and snatch out from under our feet everything we've worked hard for. And where will you be? Sitting entranced in a courtyard, painting a piece of bamboo. Yang Tzu, we'll be forced to become tenants on our own estate! Yang Tzu! Help us!" But the young artist, while sympathizing with his parent's apprehensions, was much too preoccupied with his own obsessive desire to find himself by way of paint and brush to really care about material concerns. It was not so much that his lack of filial piety was a conscious rebellion against the tenets of Confucianism; to him, it was simply a matter of priority, of values and aspirations. Yang Tzu, you see, wanted nothing less than to become the greatest artist in all of China.

He had learned, more than once, that artists are by nature selfish, that artists confine themselves within worlds that cannot be wholly shared; and though some of late had made attempts at making their art a community endeavor, Yang Tzu found isolation an absolute need. Without it he could not find himself in his art, and unlike the community efforts at painting murals, which all looked rather boring and sterile to him, he wanted his artwork to be *his* artwork. He wanted only *his* name on what *he* painted. He would not compromise *his* talents in the least for *other's* ideology. And so, invariably, the price he paid for his needed solitude was loneliness itself.

One day Yang Tzu decided to paint the town water wheel. Lo Feng, his art instructor, had informed him that it is crucial for an artist to realize the mind's tendency to paint what is not actually there. "When you paint a tree," he once told Yang Tzu, "you must remind yourself that what you are painting is an image that has no form outside your mind. You interpret, you categorize, and the reality of the tree is unavoidably distorted. Now, there are two methods of approach that I want you to explore: the first involves clearing your mind so as to mirror what it sees without discoloring it with conventional imagery. The other starts out the same way, but instead of merely reflecting onto canvas the shape of the object, attempt to capture its essence by closing the gap between the perceiver and the perceived. The results may be entirely different, yet both, in their own way, more or less accurate ... I am convinced however that neither way is capable of defining even something as deceptively simple as a rock or a block of wood. All attempts are mere distortions."

Bearing all this in mind, Yang Tzu set out to paint two versions of the water wheel — the "body" of the wheel and its "spirit". As one might suspect, the young artist soon became frustrated. His "body" painting, to the eye of the beholder, was actually an astonishing imitation of the actual. He detailed with great vividness the waterfall streaming down, the sparkling, star-like reflections of white light off the water's transparency, the splashing of the water against the wheel — which stood tall, wet, and cracked — and the grey, jagged rocks and deep, cloudless autumn sky. It might have been a photograph, so real did it seem. And so he stood upon the bank and asked himself: "Why go to all this trouble when I could have just taken a photo of it? What's the use? Is not my rendition somewhat stale and lifeless? Yet, in spite of his misgivings, he forced himself to finish the "body" version, and was left struggling to visualize how he would take up his next task to capture the spirit of the water wheel on canvas.

During the next several months, a time during which he allowed outside pressures and unseen social forces to compress and constrict his romantic view of the world, Yang Tzu rechanneled his energies, cast himself into his schoolwork, and dove headfirst into the gurgling volcano of political theory. He read books on socialism, listened to government speakers who passed through town on a crusade to "re-educate the masses", and, as if in defiance of his previous selfishness, became secretly involved in the fledgling Communist Youth Organization, for which he wrote several radically-minded articles under the pen name of Chu Wu.

The artist in him, however, was not so easily suppressed. One day, some months later when the orchard tress were beginning to blossom, he found himself sitting before the water wheel with a blank canvas in front of him. The sun, now high overhead, seemed to massage his brain with its invisible rays. The grass on the riverbank was lush and he could smell its greenness. He could see the breeze as it softly glided over him. Above, the clouds assumed shapes, which, with a little imagination, might have been taken for a herd of water buffalo charging from a dust cloud. Yang Tzu was leaning backwards to watch the buffalo slowly emerging when suddenly he felt a horrendous tug in the back of his head. He plummeted, like a rock down a well, into a strange dream where he found himself wandering through a maze whose walls were elaborately painted with a multitude of articulate scenes. There were colorful battle scenes, unending domestic and natural scenes full of men and women and animals going about their business of living. There were urban scenes, hundreds, thousands, millions of people — young, old, thin, fat, who drank, fought, laughed, read, bathed, ate, played, and travelled. It seemed to him a vast mural of the entire world, of every place and everyone in it, all of it painted impeccably.

Scanning the walls, scene after scene, alive with wonder, he turned a corner in this enormous gallery and saw a man on a ladder painting a government official who sat wistfully at his desk with his head in his hands and a dour, embittered look on his face. The painter, a young man with glasses, wore a long, paint-splotched smock. His eyes gleamed as they turned on Yang Tzu.

"I see we have a visitor," he said with feigned surprise. "Come. While you are here, I want to show you something."

Without saying a word, Yang Tzu followed the painter through the labyrinth of hallways until at last they came to a halt. "Look here," said the young man, pointing. "This is your village."

As Yang Tzu scrutinized the scene, recognizing various shops and houses, he was suddenly swallowed by a warm, rushing fear. He saw a small figure, himself, sitting before the water wheel with a blank canvas by his side. The closer he examined this scene, the more he felt himself being drawn into it, and though he tried desperately to resist, he was powerless to do so. It was like trying to fight off a heavy, impending sleep.

He closed his eyes and let go, and the instant he did there came a jolting tug in his forehead. Opening his eyes again, he found himself sitting before the revolving wheel, his brushes caressing the canvas without any mental direction on his part, without any interpretation of what he was seeing or experiencing. He knew, however, that it was his spirit, not his body, doing the painting. And with his brushes splashing rays of light across the canvas with broad, sweeping strokes, he painted what his eyes beheld as the spirit of the wheel; that is, he recorded the natural flux that occurs between the world of physical and spiritual reality, composed of an interchange of light and matter.

When at last he was done, he felt another violent tug and found himself back in the hallway with the young man in the smock. He looked at the wall. On the canvas, a swirling orb figure evoked the illusion of motion, of revolution. Yang Tzu understood only too well what he had done. It terrified him because his intellect was incapable of putting into words a description that could precipitate what it was he had seen. It could neither formulate nor crystallize. It could only distort.

The painter eyed him curiously. "We are all artists," he said. "There is not one among us who does not paint himself a picture of the world. I, for instance, painted this picture of yourself, allowing you to fill in the details. My pigments are the substance of dream, as are yours."

Yang Tzu, horrified by this implication, stammered: "Do you mean to say that you are dreaming me right now?"

"Yes, of course," the young man replied. "Just as you are dreaming me at this very moment."

Yang Tzu's more reasonable self, the dormant one, suddenly demanded an audience. He grabbed a paintbrush, dipped it into a bucket of paint, cried, "This is irrational!" and assassinated the Yang Tzu of the mural with one quick stroke. He immediately awoke from his dream in such a fright that he jumped up and upset his painting utensils. In a fit of paranoiac fear, he smashed his implements against the rocks, ripped the canvas in front of him — which had been painted and then smeared — into shreds, and gave up art forever. Later he joined the Communist government, and when his parents died, he liquidated the family estate.

Yang the artist was never seen or heard from again. Somewhere, in some distant dream, he lies buried beneath a stroke of paint. As for the village water wheel, it is broken.

The bearings went bad; and, as no one bothered to repair it, it began to rot.

Today, one may see tourists standing around snapping photos of the famous water wheel. Everyone, it seems, has heard of the acclaimed masterpiece (Yang Tzu's "body" version), which hangs in a museum in Beijing. That this painting, later retitled "The Workers Wheel" by the state art committee, is now considered a national treasure is undeniable. Moreover, many post-Revolution art critics consider Yang Tzu to be China's greatest living artist, despite the fact that he gave up painting long ago. Thus it came to pass that Yang Tzu's dream of becoming the greatest artist in all of China had become a reality, albeit an exaggerated, distorted one. Ironically, he now sits wistfully at his desk with his head in his hands and a dour, embittered look on his face — the very government bureaucrat that the young man in the smock had painted on the dream mural of life. His bitterness springs from his regret at having abandoned his artistic talent, and his realization that his fingers have grown too stiff to take up painting again. If, however, on some auspicious day, the hero of our story finds his way back into the dream labyrinth and uncovers himself from beneath the stroke of paint, I will do my best to inform you of his progress.

IV.
NEW ZEALAND

Loughlin's Trade

"Mackay, your dealing with me is very bad; I have long ago placed all this land in your hands for gold mining purposes. Let the boundary be at the termination of the land! Who originates this idea? To leave the body of the canoe in one place, and the stern piece in another?"
—Hohepa Parone Tarawerawera of the Ngatimaru tribe, March 9, 1868 address to James Mackay, Civil Commissioner of the Hauraki District, North Island, New Zealand.

I.

Loughlin was standing in his paddock, cutting manuka scrub with a slasher, when the shots rang out. He threw his gaze toward the hills, listened for a moment in silence, then whistled to his dog and wandered across the meadow to his small, one-room cabin by the banks of the Te Puru Stream. He took down his hunting rifle and pocketed some shells, then slipped on a pair of boots, donned a woolen, thread- bare cap, and headed back up the hill, his dog following closely at his feet, in search of the intruder.

They followed a footpath along a creek, stopping to rest before plunging into the subtropical bush. Here lay the limits of his own slashings — a tangled mass of fern and vine commingled with ancient stands of the giant kauri and kahikatea, trees whose seeds had sprouted before the birth of Christ. Strange birds had evolved here over the centuries, some of them wingless, but no land animals, other than the goats, pig and deer brought over by the colonists, had ever sprung to life in these isolated islands.

"Go on ahead, dog," he said, stopping to wipe the sweat from his face.

A loud crack broke over the crest of the hill. He followed the bearing of the shot for several minutes, hacking at the underbrush with a machete, until he saw, in a stand of young rimu saplings, a Maori man sitting alone by the carcass of a deer.

"Oi!" he called out. "What are you doing here? You're on private property."

The Maori, a fierce-looking Polynesian with a broad face, glared indignantly at Loughlin. "Private property? Well, that's a laugh. This isn't your land, Pakeha."

Loughlin approached cautiously, his rifle leveled at the chest of the native. "Listen, mate. I do own this patch of land. I bought it four months ago. Two hundred acres in all, from the tops of these hills and on down to the river. I've got the papers to prove it."

A wry smile crossed the Maori's face. "Well, that sounds pretty official. But I think you got buggered, European."

Loughlin lowered his rifle. "I bought this land from an agent of the Kauri Timber Company. I've got the bloody deed. Now do me a favor and bugger off!"

"No. The Kauri Timber Company owns no title to this land," the Maori calmly replied. "They once had a lease on the timber rights, but it expired a few months ago. I should know. I'm the one that leased it to them."

The image of the land agent, Russek — the little man with the uneven mustache — sprang into Loughlin's mind, confirming the vague suspicions that he had managed to bury for so long.

"For all I know, you're both bloody liars. Get over here dog!" Loughlin commanded. His companion, having sensed something in the bush, returned to his master's side.

The Maori, a stout, bare-chested, muscular man, leaned his back against a tree trunk, laid his rifle by the deer, and placed his rough, calloused hands on top of his knees, displaying an almost regal confidence and pride. "Be careful how you choose your words, Pakeha," he said. "A Maori never forgets an insult."

This matter of fact show of confidence unnerved Loughlin, who had never before been challenged by a Maori.

"Who are you?" he asked. "What's your name?"

"Hona Pau," the Maori said. He held out a canteen of water, and motioned for Loughlin to sit. He studied the white man for a moment, and said: "Look. I'm getting tired of fighting with you Europeans. I'm not promising you anything right now. But I reckon maybe we can work something out."

Loughlin, realizing that he had no money to offer the Maori, said: "S'pose you're right. S'pose it turns out I was buggered — and I'm not admitting that I was. What kind of an arrangement might you be willing to consider?"

Hona Pau stood up. He grabbed the deer by the hoofs and slung it over his shoulder with a grunt. "Well, I'll let you know, " he replied, giving Loughlin's dog a scratch on the back. "Give us a few days to think it over, eh?" He nodded brusquely at Loughlin, turned his broad back on the white man, and broke into a chant as he strode through the bush, stooping, now and then, to study the animal tracks that he spied in the soft, dark, humid earth.

II.

A dull blue haze, fed by the gaseous eruptions of industrial and household chimneys, enveloped the coastal town sites of Thames and Grahamstown. Goldfield batteries, crushing precious ore with clockwork rhythm, boomed ominously from the nearby claims, and the hills themselves, once covered with a healthy skin of subtropical forest, stood slashed and scarred, criss-crossed with a latticework of tramways and roads and water supply flumes. Red soil, tailing heaps, and giant pumps now dotted the sea-side range—an ugly, unnatural wreckage speckled with tents and shacks and crowded with the thousands of miners who trekked down from the hills every Saturday night to fill the pubs, hotels, theaters, and whorehouses in their checkered shirts and mole-skin trousers. People thronged down the muddy footpaths now, slogging back and forth on their way to work: men, women, uniformed schoolchildren, edging their way along the rimu boardwalks.

"Mr. Loughlin," the lawyer said, frowning at his guest, whose tattered, patch-kneed pantaloons and muddied hob-nailed boots he evidently considered offensive. "You know who Jerome Throckmorton is. Mr. Mackay, of course, is our Civil Commissioner."

"Sure," said Stuart Loughlin. "I've worked in Mr. Throckmorton's mine at Waiotahi Creek. I'm glad to finally meet you," he said, rising slightly in his chair and nodding to the gentlemen by the window.

"Glad to know you, Loughlin," said Throckmorton, returning a smile.

"Your honor," Loughlin said, addressing the Commissioner. "I have a complaint I'd like to make, sir, against a man named Russek. He swindled me out of three hundred pounds on a land transaction."

"Yes," the Commissioner said. "We know about Russek."

"Then I s'pose I've no legal deed to the land I paid him for."

"No," replied the Commissioner. "I'm afraid you don't." He cast a furtive glance at Throckmorton, who was lighting himself a cigar. "However, there may be some light at the end of the tunnel. In fact, this case has some bearing on the issue we had in mind."

"How's that, sir?"

Throckmorton came to the fore. He stood before Loughlin, adjusted his spectacles, and said: "You know a Maori chief named Hona Pau?"

"Yeh. I met him in the bush not long ago. He was the one that told me I'd been swindled. Claims the land is his."

"Well, it is," Throckmorton replied gruffly. "Along with thousands of other acres which he refuses to lease to us. This Pau's a difficult man, harbors a deep-seated hatred against whites. His uncle was a signatory to the Treaty of Waitangi, you know, which most Maoris now consider to be a sell-out to the British Crown."

The Commissioner cleared his throat. "Several years ago," he said, addressing Loughlin in a smooth, sleepy voice, "I held an appointment in the South Island as Native Assistant Secretary for the Government. When I came to the Thames area I learned that the Maoris, who had never surrendered their rebellion against the Crown, had decided that they wanted to stop the fighting. I made a recommendation to the Colonial Secretary in Auckland that a Magistrate be appointed for this district, and that his duties should include bringing about mineral and timber lease agreements with the natives, there being some small finds in the area at this point in time. When I myself was appointed Civil Commissioner, I undertook to persuade the natives that it was in their own best interest to make such leases, but was opposed by Hona Pau's father. Eventually we persuaded most of the Hauraki area tribes to make leases on blocks surrounding his father's land, and the rest, as they say, is history.

"Hona Pau's father died last year, leaving Pau the new chief. Unfortunately he's very much like his father — stingy and mistrustful — and so he's continued to hold out, leasing only a few small blocks from his vast land holdings on the Coromandel Peninsula. Now, Mr. Throckmorton here has done some surveying on some of this land, and has some reason to believe there is an economic gold-bearing deposit in the vicinity of your present home."

Stuart Loughlin's eyes grew wide. "Ah, well. Imagine that," he said. "Gold on me own property."

"The land's not yours, Loughlin," Throckmorton replied, cutting his eyes sharply at the Commissioner.

"No. Evidently not," said Loughlin.

"We sympathize with you, Mr. Loughlin," said Mackay, "and will do everything we can to get you your money back. In the meantime, however, Mr. Throckmorton has a proposal for you."

Throckmorton put his hand on Loughlin's shoulder, patted it paternally, and paced back and forth in front of him. "Hona Pau has a great dislike for many of the mining companies in this region," he said. "He claims we've ravaged the land without restoring it and have systematically cheated the other tribes out of their fair share of royalties. This is utter rubbish, mind you. We've always been just with the natives; it's in our best interest to do so. Nevertheless, there's more than money involved here. Hona Pau is a fiercely proud man, and has always resented the intrusion of Europeans onto his land. On the bright side, he's been willing to make a few small land sales to settlers, such as yourself, including the right to prospect for minerals. In short, he won't deal with us: to him we represent everything that he despises about white men. But he might deal with you, especially since you've been so grievously duped — something that, as a Maori, he can relate too. Because of this, we think it likely Pau will sympathize with you and accept a reasonable offer for the land." Mr. Throckmorton threw his gaze to the lawyer, Hoffsteader, who frowned at Loughlin as if to make a point of his dislike for him.

"Mr. Throckmorton has agreed to provide you with the cash for the sale of the land," the lawyer said officiously. "The land will be yours, the title being legally placed in your name. Once this is done, you will in turn assign to us the mineral rights to the acreage. If you agree with these terms, then sign this document, which spells out the conditions in greater detail."

Loughlin twisted his cap in his hands for a moment. "So. What you are offering is a trade. I get the land, and you get the gold."

"Subject to any royalty clauses in the contract to Hona Pau," said the lawyer.

After mulling it over for several minutes, Loughlin agreed to the proposed terms, though it was evident from his expression that he felt somehow cheated by this arrangement. Hoffsteader drew up four copies of the agreement, which were then signed by all parties, including the lawyer, who evidently had an interest in the arrangement. Loughlin didn't understand all the archaic, circuitous language in the agreement, and when he asked for a clarification on one of the more nonsensical legal phrases, he was frowned at by Hoffsteader, who proceeded to give Loughlin an equally archaic, circuitous explanation of the legal terminology, sprinkling his lecture with words like "indemnification" and other such mysterious terms. In the end, Loughlin signed the document, making some pretense of having understood its language, and was given a copy. Throckmorton nodded at Commissioner Mackay, and walked out of the office without once glancing in Loughlin's direction. The Commissioner, for his part, mustered a slightly condescending nod, while the lawyer Hoffsteader managed to lift the edges of his mouth in a supercilious little smile, as if to say: "You're lucky we gave you anything at all."

III.

It was a sunny summer day. Not a cloud in the sky. Loughlin tipped his cap at an old woman who shunted him aside with her parasol, and walked down Arthur Street. As he neared Scrip Corner he was suddenly confronted by a thin, bony figure with unwashed hair, narrow eyes and blockish face. The man had just exited the Exchange, and was walking briskly under the veranda amidst the share brokers who strolled up and down the street, crying out stock prices and selling shares on the spot. When the figure turned and looked up, Loughlin immediately recognized him: it was that little bastard thief, Bernard Russek.

"How ya going, mate?" Loughlin said, grabbing Russek by the arm as he attempted to pass him on the boardwalk. "Let's have a chin-wag, shall we?"

"Oh, g'day, Loughlin," Russek stammered. "Fancy running into you here. I've been meaning to get out to your place; but I've been so busy, you know, it just hasn't been possible. Seems there's a problem with the deed to your property."

"Aw, yeh?" Loughlin said, pulling Russek down the walk.

"I've got important business, Loughlin."

"Well then. Let's go in here and have a cup of tea, and discuss some important business."

Loughlin pulled Russek into a small restaurant and bar called "The Moa", run by an amiable Maori cook called Maaka. A large wood sign hung down over the door. On it was a carving of one of the giant Moas — a flightless emu-like bird unique to New Zealand — that the Maori hunted to extinction before the Pakeha arrived.

"G'day, Maaka," Loughlin said, saluting the Maori behind the bar.

"Ah, g'day, Stu. How ya going, mate? I thought they'd buried you in the mines."

"No, no. I've moved up a bit in the world, as you can plainly see." He held out his arms for the Maori to admire his new suit.

"Pah! Bit too posh, boy. You getting married today?"

"Hardly. Bring us some tea, will ya?"

"Righto, mate. Two teas it is." Maaka put a kettle on the stove.

"Sit down, Mr. Russek," Loughlin said. "I hope you feel like talking. Cuz if you don't, I'll break out every bloody tooth in your head."

"All right, all right," Russek said. "Look. I'm really sorry about your money."

"Sure ya are. Now start talking."

"All right. I'll tell you whatever you want to know. Just don't break out my teeth."

"Where's me money," Loughlin demanded.

"It's gone."

"Gone where."

"Invested."

"Invested in what?"

"Well," said Russek, running his fingers through his hair. "It's like this, Mr. Loughlin. I work for a bloke named Carvey, right? Carvey's a land broker. He buys land from the Maoris. Gives them a few quid, and makes them think they're lucky. Then he resells it to settlers, farmers, you know, people new to the area, at inflated prices. Well. He piled up some money over the years, and began speculating with it, financing small mining tributes, that kind of thing. Then he started getting into cash flow problems, so he took to selling land that wasn't legally his to sell. I didn't want to get involved. Really I didn't. But I'm in hock to him up to my ears, and there was nothing I could bloody do. Please don't turn me in, sir. I can get you your money back. Maybe untold more."

"How d'ya mean."

Maaka brought over the tea.

"Tah, mate," Loughlin said to the Maori.

"Carvey owns a lot of claims," Russek said quietly. "He usually turns them to publicly traded mining companies and retains an interest in the form of shares. Several years ago, he traded an undeveloped claim for shares in the Union

138

Jack mine, which today pays out no dividends, and is virtually shutdown. Only one miner, Tom Hamilton, works it now; and he hates old Carvey, who's buggered him over in the past. Well, what Carvey doesn't know yet is that Tom, who's working a new drive tunnel, just bored into a huge reef patch. It looks very promising. Here. Have a look." Russek reached into his pocket and handed Loughlin a fist-sized piece of quartz studded with gold.

"I know Tom Hamilton," Loughlin said, studying the ore. "Good joker. As honest a man as I've ever met. Did he give you this?"

"Yes. Only an hour ago. I was in the mine. He showed me the reef."

"Has he told Carvey about it yet?"

"I was on my way to tell him about it when you grabbed me."

"What were you doing at the Exchange then?"

Russek looked around the room to make sure no one could hear. "That's the good news, Mr. Loughlin. Carvey put his shares in the mine on the market three months ago, and he hasn't had any buyers. Why should he? The mine's not paying any dividends, and the area is considered to have small potential. He owns 3,500 shares in this claim, and there's plenty more for sale on the market. The value of the shares is peanuts, but in an hour or two you won't be able to buy them at any price."

"How much do they sell for now?"

"Eight pence a share. Tom and I just purchased one hundred shares between us," added Russek, "which was all we could afford. Have a look." He showed Loughlin the stock receipts he had just picked up at the Exchange. "You won't tell Carvey we bought these shares before we notified him, will ya? I'm in enough bloody trouble as it is."

Loughlin laughed. "Don't worry about that, boy. Come on. You and me is going to pay ole Tom Hamilton a visit."

IV.

The two men mounted their horses and rode two miles south along the main thoroughfare. They turned east on a footpath, heading straight into the hills, and followed a swath of cleared ground littered with wood planks and tailing piles. For twenty minutes they clopped along through the muddy, disheveled earth, until at last they stood on an elongated spur, which overlooked the town below. It was midday by now; the sun bore down on them heavily, soaking them in sweat and burning the backs of their necks.

Russek dismounted and led Loughlin to the opening of the steeply dipping shaft. A whim barrel pulled by a horse had been set up to raise ore from the ground; from here the ore was transported to one of the nearby batteries for processing.

"Oi! Tom! It's me! Russek!"

In a few minutes a man in muddied clothes appeared. "Hey," he said suspiciously. "What are you doing back here?"

"G'day, Tom," Loughlin said.

"Oh. Hello, Stu. How are ya, mate?" The bearded man stepped out of the shaft and shook hands with Loughlin. "You must be looking for work, eh? Well I'm afraid you won't find any here, mate. This ole ground's been milked for all she's worth, I reckon. Wouldn't pay for the grease for the wagon wheels."

"It's all right. He knows," said Russek.

Tom made a face. "Knows what?"

"This joker bilked me out of three hundred pounds on a land sale," Loughlin said.

Tom laughed. "Carvey buggered ya, did he? Well. I'm not surprised. He's a sneaky little bastard. Anyway, I'm not on social terms with his lackey here. He just happen to come along at an inopportune moment, if you follow me."

"Here's your shares," Russek said, handing Tom a receipt for the stock certificates.

"So what have you found down there, mate?" Loughlin asked. "A leader? A shoot maybe?"

Tom broke out into a broad smile. "No, mate," he said, handing him a candle. "It's a bloody great patch. And it's chock full of gold."

Loughlin and Hamilton lighted their candles in the entrance of the mineshaft and sloshed through the ankle-deep water that covered the floor, crouching as they went, until they reached the end of the primary tunnel. Here they found several branches, known as drive tunnels, which broke off perpendicular to the main shaft in an attempt to locate the so-called reefs of gold. Tom led them into one of these drives and they followed it for approximately fifty feet, the light of their candles illuminating the wet, narrow walls as they trudged along in a crouch. Finally they turned off into another branch, and within a few minutes they were standing before the dead end of the tunnel where the floor lay strewn with the loose rock dislodged by Tom's early morning dynamite blasts.

Loughlin held up his candle by the wall of rock, and swore in wonder at the sight before him. The entire wall was streaked with thick gold-filled bands that criss-crossed the quartz rock host in spectacular patterns. A few of the veins were impregnated with solid gold with diameters the thickness of rope strands. The matrix of the quartz itself was richly interspersed with gold grain. In all his years of mining, Loughlin had never seen anything like it.

"She's a beauty, isn't she?" Tom said proudly. "Now it's only a matter of following her footsteps as far as the lease boundaries. Too bad the eastern boundary is so close — only twenty feet away, I reckon."

"Yeh," Loughlin said. "That's too bad. What's the next block over then?"

"That would be the Top Heavy lease," Tom said. He held up his candle in front of Loughlin and eyed him with a steady glare. "Listen, Stuart," he said quietly. "I think you're a decent sort of bloke, so I'm going to let you in on a little secret. The Top Heavy shaft never made it to the main fault where all the gold reefs are found. It was one of the early crosscuts in these hills, so the owners were probably never even aware of the fault's existence. Since then there have been two other mines on this hill — the Colonial and the Elizabeth — that have tapped into the reefs. Both of them pulled out over two million in gold and are still going along at a nice little trot. The owners of this mine here have been searching for this fault; and well, now you're looking at it. I reckon there's more than a million in gold in this patch, assuming there's any size to it at all, and another million or more in the Top Heavy block twenty feet away from where we now stand. The beauty of it is, that lease is now open."

"What?"

"Ay. She's free and clear. And here's the gist of it: I can't do this all by myself. I need a partner who can put up some money for the lease. It's a good omen, I reckon, the way you fell into this deal: you and I have broken our picks together in these god-forsaken wormholes for years now, and I know you're a trustworthy sort. So I'm asking you now, are you in a position to buy the lease?"

Loughlin thought for a minute. "Yes," he said. "Don't worry. I've got the money."

"Then," said Tom, "what do you say we go in as equal partners. Can you live with that, mate?"

"Sure. I reckon that's fair," said Loughlin. "Just keep that little bastard Russek out of it."

"Not to worry," said Hamilton, extending his hand and consummating the arrangement with a strong handshake. "He's not aware of the particulars of the block next to us. The problem is, we've got to secure that lease before word gets out about the discovery here at the Union Jack. Otherwise, we haven't got a chance."

"That'll be difficult," Loughlin admitted. "Who owns the land?"

"A company here in town, Throckmorton Mines. They bought it twelve years ago from the Maoris, and it was Throckmorton who drove the crosscut shaft which never reached the fault. Since then they've had no operations on the lease, and I expect they consider the land a barren prospect. I'm sure they would lease it out."

"What time is it now?"

Tom pulled out his pocket watch. "Half past eleven."

"Good," Loughlin said. "I want you to hoist the flag over the whim-head at half past three to announce the find. I should have everything taken care of by then, and the brokers at the Exchange will see the signal before they close up the trading."

"Fine," Tom said. "Now let's get out of this blinking shit-hole before you ruin that dandy little suit of yours."

V.

"Back so soon, Mr. Loughlin?" Hoffsteader asked. He looked up at the miner from behind his mahogany desk as he hastily thumbed through a pile of documents. "I trust you plan on making a good impression on the native, Hona Pau?"

"Well. As a matter of fact I've already spoken with Pau," Loughlin said. "And he indicated that he may be interested in selling the land."

"Ah," said the lawyer. He cast aside his papers. "Well. What exactly did he say?"

Loughlin took a seat and casually smoothed the wrinkles of his trouser leg. "He said he thought three hundred was a fair price. But he was a little mistrustful, as if he doubted that I had that kind of money."

"Good news. Mr. Throckmorton will be ecstatic." Hoffsteader glared fixedly at Loughlin, his oblong, whiskered face accommodating a selfish measure of gratitude and respect. Loughlin's new appearance, and the way he carried himself in his new suit of clothes, had evidently made a favorable impression on the lawyer.

"When do you think we can close on this, Mr. Loughlin? Today, possibly?"

Loughlin put his hands behind the back of his head and thought for a moment. "I don't know. It's possible I s'pose. But you never know with these Maoris. They have a tendency to back out on you at the last minute."

"Yes, I'm aware of that. It's given me untold headaches. A deal is never done with them until all the contracts have been signed. And even then they keep pestering you for more."

"I think it might help if I were to dangle the money in front of him. You know, it might entice him into signing the contract."

"Of course. I agree. I'll draw up a check immediately." Hoffsteader took out his checkbook and wrote out a check for three hundred pounds. He tore it off ceremoniously, and handed it to Loughlin.

"Here you are. Let me know if he wants more. We can go a bit higher if he starts getting greedy. But let me warn you, Mr. Loughlin. This money is for the purchase of that land, and if I find out you've undercut Mr. Throckmorton on the purchase price and pocketed the difference, I'll make sure that he knows about it. Do we understand one another?"

"Yes, sir," Loughlin said. "We do."

"Very well, then. Good day. And good luck to you. Let me know the outcome as soon as possible."

Loughlin nodded. "There's just one other matter I'd like your help on, Mr. Hoffsteader."

The lawyer looked at him impatiently. "Yes? What is it, man?"

"There's some land a friend of mine is interested in the Kauaeranga area. He says that Throckmorton Mines owns the land, and when I told him that I was on good terms with Mr. Throckmorton, he asked me to purchase a lease on it for him. Said if I could get the lease, he'd like for it to be put in both our names as consideration for me getting it for him."

"You didn't mention our arrangement with this fellow, did you? You do realize how confidential a matter this is?"

"Of course," Loughlin assured him. "I said nothing about that. That would be contrary to my own best interests, now wouldn't it?"

"You're learning, Mr. Loughlin," the lawyer replied cynically. "Where is this property exactly?"

"It's the old Top Heavy lease, about two miles south, in the hills off the coast road."

Hoffsteader sat back in his chair and thought for a moment. "What does he want with it," he said suspiciously. "Has he found anything there?"

"I don't think so. There's never been anything found in that area and I don't expect there ever will be. But you know how these fellows are. Optimistic to a fault, some of them. He probably wants to pan the stream, that sort of thing."

"I don't think we are leasing out any holdings now," the lawyer said. "Maybe he should look elsewhere for his gold."

At that moment Throckmorton entered the room.

"Mr. Loughlin," he said gruffly. "I'm surprised to see you back here so soon. Have you talked to Pau?"

Loughlin told him that he had, and proceeded to repeat to Throckmorton the story he had told the lawyer. The news of this progress had a noticeable effect on Throckmorton. He paced about the room, agitated and distracted to the point of talking to himself.

Loughlin brought up the issue of the Top Heavy. "It's a favor for an old mate of mine, Mr. Throckmorton. But Mr. Hoffsteader here doesn't think you want to make any leases."

"Nonsense," Throckmorton said. "We make them all the time. We can't explore all our properties by ourselves, you know. And besides, we gave up on the Top Heavy a long time ago. Your friend is probably wasting his time."

"I'm aware of that, sir. I told him it was a barren lease. But he's a bit hard-headed, and insisted on me talking to you about it."

"All right. Mr. Hoffsteader. Make up a lease. Charge him five pounds." He walked over to Loughlin and shook his hand vigorously. "I obviously underestimated you, Loughlin," he said with a smile.

"Forget it," Loughlin replied. "If I were you I probably would've done the same."

VI.

Stuart Loughlin took the check for three hundred pounds to the Bank of New Zealand and deposited it into his account. He then walked over to Scrip Corner—a conglomeration of share broker offices set up under a long veranda on the southern side of Arthur Street. Young men with handlebar mustaches stood outside the Exchange office, quote sheets in hand, yelling out stock prices like fishmongers announcing the price of cod or whale meat. Thousands of shares of gold and timber stocks traded daily at this corner, named for the "scrip" stock, which floated start-up companies hungry for capital to develop their holdings. Loughlin could see speculators perched upon the balconies of the hotels overlooking the corner, sipping tea and waiting for incoming news from the mines. He was aware that a covert communication system had been set up, whereby if gold were discovered in the hills overlooking the town sites, a speculator might, for instance, spy coded semaphore signals — formed by arranging the arms in letter shapes — that signified the type of find that had been made. Otherwise, a flag might be raised if a "reef" were discovered. Loughlin looked southward, and could just make out the top of the whim of the Union Jack, where Tom would raise the signal in a matter of minutes.

Loughlin entered the Exchange, and purchased 3,750 shares in the Union Jack concern at 3:23 p.m. He paid a total of three hundred pounds for the shares.

He wandered over to the Palace Hotel across the street and got a room for the night overlooking Scrip Corner. He sat out on the balcony in a wicker chair with several other speculators, lit his pipe, and watched as the tiny flag went up the whim at the Union Jack mine.

Within minutes, the share brokers on the streets were calling out: "Reef flag at the Union Jack! Reef flag at the Union Jack! Price at eight pence!"

Several men jumped on their horses and barreled south on Arthur Street, heading for the mine. Meanwhile, the surrounding offices poured out share brokers, investment analysts, bankers, journalists, clerks, managers and executives, who congregated in the streets around the Exchange, craning their necks over the gathering crowd and pushing to get into the Exchange building. At first no one seemed willing to believe that the old Union Jack mine, which had been around for over twelve years, had suddenly hit a patch reef. But then Russek rode in, announcing with shouts and waves of his hat that the strike was a legitimate gold reef. With the news of the discovery confirmed, an orgy of speculation began.

At 3:40, the brokers cried out: "Reef flag at the Union Jack! Price at three pounds."

At 4:10, a tremendous crowd had gathered at Scrip Corner, pushing their way toward the young share brokers, yelling that they wanted to buy stock in the Union Jack.

"Fifty shares at six and a shilling," yelled a broker on a trade.

A woman who stood on the balcony near Loughlin cried out for 300 shares, for which she paid over ten pounds a share, and was relieved when one of the young brokers caught her cry and flicked his wrist, indicating that the sale had been made.

At 4:40, a rider came galloping down the street, yelling: "It's a reef! And it looks like the Colonial!"

Hearing this, the crowd grew anxious, and bid the price up even higher.

"Sixty shares at twelve and sixpence," came a share broker's cry.

"One hundred and twenty-five shares at fifteen pounds."

Finally, by the end of the trading day, the stock closed at just under twenty-three pounds a share, so that, in the span of a little over an hour, Stuart Loughlin had made a paper profit of approximately eighty-five thousand pounds.

VII.

Loughlin awoke early the next morning, drank two cups of tea in the hotel bar, walked across the street to the Exchange, and sold fourteen of his shares in the Union Jack. He then mounted his horse and rode down Pollen Street into the Thames township, dismounting at the offices of Throckmorton Mines, Ltd.

He found Jerome Throckmorton sitting at his desk, reading the *Thames Gazette* and drinking tea.

"Good morning," said Loughlin, removing his hat.

Throckmorton frowned. "Well, if it isn't the illustrious Stuart Loughlin. I hear you're quite a speculator now."

Loughlin put his hands behind his back and wandered over to the window by Throckmorton's desk. "I've been known to gamble now and then," he admitted.

"With money that isn't yours?"

Loughlin looked out quietly into the street.

"That's a foolish way to make your living," Throckmorton went on. "I suppose you're now going to try and resell me the Top Heavy lease for some ridiculous amount of money. If so, I'm afraid you're wasting both my time and yours."

"No," said Loughlin. "I'm here on another matter."

"And what might that be?"

"To let you know that the negotiation for Pau's land fell through after all." He took out an envelope from his coat pocket and tossed it on Throckmorton's desk. "Here's your three hundred pounds. Plus the extra ten that you gave me. Pau said he'd decided that it wasn't in his own best interests to sell the land at this time. So. I reckon that's the end of it."

Throckmorton leaned back in his chair and stared fixedly at Loughlin. He opened his mouth as if to speak, but instead shook his head dismissively.

"Something on your mind?" Loughlin asked.

"No. Not really. Just a thought — something an old Maori once told me on a land transaction. He said they believe that a man is only as good as his word."

"Yeh," Loughlin said, putting on his hat. "I reckon that's why they think so poorly of blokes like us, eh?"

Throckmorton laughed. "Maybe so. In any event, I think our business has come to an end. You were lucky, Loughlin. Lucky, and just plain foolish."

Stuart Loughlin said good day, and rode back to his farm by the Te Puru Stream. He gazed in fascination at the beauty of the pristine hills where, in stark contrast to the hills behind the townships, no cutting of trees or gouging of tunnels or building of tramways had been done. There was a wildness to this isolated valley, a primitive, aboriginal richness whose natural grandeur belittled the artificial monuments and machinery of the Pakeha. There would be no mineshafts or logging camps in the hills surrounding his farm, not if he could help it. Let it stay as he'd found it, unadulterated, immune from the reach of men like Throckmorton and Mackay. That he was, in many ways, no different from these men did not escape his own scrutiny: It motivated him to probe for the roots of his own avarice, and come to terms, as did Throckmorton, with the irreparable damage that he had inflicted on his own integrity — damage that would never be mitigated by the fact that he had made himself, by virtue of his own deceit, one of the richest men in the borough of Thames.

He saw Hona Pau one day, walking down the coastal road on his way into town. He greeted the Maori, and asked him whether he had settled on an arrangement, a lease perhaps, for him to stay on the land that he now occupied.

"Yeh," Pau said. "I've been giving it a good deal of thought. And I've decided to sell it."

Loughlin glared at the native with an almost visceral agitation. "Wait a minute," he said. "I've got the money. All right? I can pay you today, in cash if you like."

The Maori frowned and shook his head. "No," he said somberly. "I'm not selling any land to you, Loughlin."

For a moment, Stuart Loughlin returned to his nervous stare, looking strangely desperate, even childishly remorse — until, regaining a sort of lurid composure, he smiled, his face now taking on an unmistakable mark of obsequiousness, an ingratiating courtesy, a smile without justification, which now rose naturally to his lips.

"You had the money for the land," Hona Pau reprimanded him, "and still you refused to offer it to me. I can't trust you anymore."

"Now wait a minute," Loughlin said, taking the tone of someone who would fix everything right, whose efficacy was beyond reproach. But before he could finish, Hona Pau said:

"The lawyer. He told me that he loaned you the money."

"What lawyer? Hoffsteader?"

"Yeh, Hoffsteader. He asked me if you'd ever made me an offer on this piece of land. He said you came begging him for a loan of three hundred quid to pay for it. And when I told him you hadn't made me any offer, he swears out loud, and then he starts to laugh; and then he offers me four hundred for the land."

A sullen look replaced the smile on Loughlin's face. He held the Maori's eyes for a moment longer, and when Hona Pau looked away, he sighed and gave a gloomy little nod, as if he'd just heard the news, and was resigned to the outcome, of the death of an old friend.

Maori Land

A breeze swept over the Firth of Thames, across the mudflats, where a young Maori waded ankle-deep along the shore. He was tall, heavy for his sixteen years, yet agile, for all his bulk, carrying himself with swift, confident movements as he scoured the flats, scooping up oysters and stabbing at flounder with his bone-handled knife. His wiry hair stuck out in every direction, forming a large ball around his head, and his brown, piercing eyes shone with an innocent yet intelligent curiosity, as though amazement came naturally to him, as though the turbid, youthful cynicism so often emergent at such an age — and so easily mirrored in the eyes — were entirely foreign to his experience.

An old flat bed Ford pulled off the coastal road and honked. "Oi!" yelled the driver.

Graeme Turoa waved, held up his sack of shellfish and shook it triumphantly.

"All right, that's enough. Now get in the truck."

"Why? What's the rush?"

"I'm bloody hungry!"

Graeme trudged over to the truck, dragging the catch bag behind him. His father's knotted biceps hung out over the window; he was glaring at Graeme from behind the wheel, goosing the accelerator with his cleated football shoes. His face was slightly bruised on one cheek.

"Got thirty-three oysters and twenty paua," Graeme said.

"Aw, yeh?"

"Easy tucker, eh? Just bend down and scoop'm up."

"Not bad, mate. We'll have a fine bit o' tea with that."

The truck sputtered down the metalled road, rounding the bends, snaking the steep, subtropical hills which jutted from the sea and made home to rare, ageless giants of the forest, like the great kauri, whose timber was once logged to the edge of extinction. Now and then the remnants of old tailing fans came into view, scars left by gold prospectors long ago, or patches of hillside cleared by farmers who continually slashed and struggled against the native growth in order to graze sheep and cattle, to build homes and raise families. In the last one hundred years the Pakeha settlers had eaten voraciously the fruits of the isolated, Eden-like islands of New Zealand, and as a result their presence was now an indelible part of the landscape.

Graeme and his father entered the village of Porua, and headed inland up a dirt road alongside the Whakahau River.

"So, how was the game, Dad?"

"We won. Twenty-four to nothing."

"Good on ya."

"Yeh. Bunch of wankers, those Whitianga blokes."

Graeme laughed, reached over and prodded his father's cheek. "Looks like one of those wankers popped you one in the eye though, eh?"

A scowl lit Colin Turoa's face. "Yeh. Some bastard elbowed me. I got even though in the next scrum. Thumped him one in the ribs, accidentally of course. They took'm out on a stretcher."

A few miles down the road they rounded a turn and beheld the local landmark, Otanui, a mountain of basalt whose somber crest of unvegetated rock now stood bathed in the early evening sun.

"Look. There's McKenzie. Looking worried, as usual."

Near the river, at the base of a cleared hill covered with a carpet of bright green grass, stood a small wood frame home surrounded by sheds and storage tanks and a fenced-in vegetable garden, all of which, including a portion of the hills beyond view, comprised the whole of the McKenzie farm. Turoa's place adjoined Ian McKenzie's, but was not so large as his neighbor's, which spread much deeper into the bush, into the wild growth where no domestic animal or man could be found.

McKenzie stood by a wooden gate in a small paddock with a hammer in hand. He was a thin man, had a thin man face, a long, hooked nose, and a shock of curly brown hair on top of his bulbous head. He stood in faded gray shorts and gumboots.

"G'day, Ian," Graeme's father said.

"G'day, Colin," McKenzie returned dolefully.

"What's up, mate?"

McKenzie tucked the hammer under his arm and held out his blistered palms.

Colin Turoa laughed. "Been cuttin' scrub, eh?"

"Yeh," said McKenzie, clenching and unclenching his fingers. "Hey, Turoa. You know a bloke named Jim Rangi?"

"Jim Rangi? No. Don't think so, mate."

"Naw. Me neither. When I was up the hill with the slasher I look up and see this big Maori bloke come stridin' out of the bush with a giant dead pig on his back. Gave me the creeps the way he came out, all quiet like."

"A Captain Cooker?" Graeme asked.

"Yeh, mate. A bloody great Captain Cook boar, black as a lump a' coal. Pongs like a rubbish dump, and is as big an' fat an' ugly as me last wife, Anabelle. Anyway, I seen that he'd been hunting back in the bush, and I asked him where he got the pig. The bloke didn't say nothin'. Just stood there with this damned pig on his back, the blood runnin' out all over'm. I noticed he didn't have a gun, or even a bow and arrow, so when I asked'm how he managed to bag the bugger he says he baited it with a loaf of bread. I says 'You what?' And he says he baited it with a loaf of bread at the base of a totara tree."

"Blimey," Graeme said.

"'Ya make a pit?' I says. And he says, 'Naw. I didn't make no pit. I just waited roun' back of the tree till he comes. Then I clubbed'm with a macrocarpa branch.'"

Colin Turoa laughed. "This Rangi joker?"

"Yeh. He's in the shed right now, cleaning the bloody pig. I told him I didn't take kindly to poachers and trespassers, and he agreed to cut me some of the meat for sausage."

"You reckon he'll sell us some?" Graeme asked.

"I don't know, boy. Go an' ask'm."

Graeme and his father parked the truck and strode into McKenzie's dark shearing shed where they found a man in a green Swanndri bush shirt, a heavy woolen garment that laced in the front and hung down to the tops of the knees. The shirt was tied at the waist with a leather belt upon which hung a large, sheathed hunting knife. His hair was pulled back into a ponytail; his face had been tattooed with swirling Maori designs, giving him a ferocious, war-like demeanor. Without glancing at either Graeme or his father, without acknowledging their presence in any way, he unsheathed his broad-bladed hunting knife and summarily stabbed it into the belly of the dead boar.

"G'day," said Colin. "Name's Colin Turoa. This is me boy, Graeme."

"G'day," the man said.

"Jesus," Graeme said, grabbing his nose. "The bastard pongs, eh?"

Rangi turned to look at them. "Yeh. He's a smelly bastard all right. But he's tasty enough when cooked."

"You from around here, mate?" Colin asked.

"No. Not originally. I'm livin' back in the hills now though, in the cabin of a relative."

"My place is over there," said Colin Turoa, jutting his chin in the direction of his house. "Graeme and me, we give it a go every now and then in these hills. Eh, Graeme? But we seldom bag any boar."

Rangi was silent. His bloodied hands were buried inside the cavity of the animal. "Your place go as far back as those old kauri on the other side of the ravine up there?" Rangi asked.

"Yeh. All the way up to the falls."

Rangi rubbed his chin with his sleeve. "Then I reckon I killed this pig on your land," he said, "and not on state land after all. I apologize for killing it, Turoa. Tell you what though. I'll clean and quarter'm for you if you'll overlook the poach and let me keep enough tucker for supper."

Surprise overcame Colin Turoa. Pleasant surprise. He strode closer to Rangi and held out his hand. "Pleased to know you, Rangi. McKenzie told me that's your name. As far as the pig goes, he's yours, mate. You bloody killed'm. And from what I hear, you did a cracker of a job, too."

"Well," said Rangi, his voice quiet, even, steady. "I'll tell you what, mate. We'll share the meat. Eh? You and me, that is. As for McKenzie, who tried to exact a toll on me, thinking I'd intentionally poached on his place, I don't reckon I'll be payin' his Pakeha tax after all, especially seein' how it was on your land and not his that I killed the pig on."

"Let's have a hangi," Graeme said. "We can throw in the shellfish that I caught."

Colin Turoa broke out in a grin. "What d'ya reckon, mate? Gut the boar and we'll throw'm into the pit with the rest of the tucker."

"We'll stuff an apple in its mouth," Graeme said.

Rangi's tattooed face broke out in a smile. "All right then," he said. "Let's give it a go."

* * *

Graeme Turoa stood by the fire in the back paddock, watching the coals heat the rounded stream cobbles that would later be buried with the meat in the hangi pit. The sheep nibbled mindlessly on the hillside nearby, bleating now and then strange, almost human utterances. The dusk had settled in. The codlin moths flew in futile, endless circlings about the porch light.

Rangi appeared, stood quietly by the fire.

"Won't be long now," Graeme said.

"Right, mate. Just came out for a durry." He took out a Rothman's cigarette and lit it. "Your father," he said, flicking away his match, "asked me to help out around here: dig a new rubbish pit, cut wood for the winter, other odd jobs that need doin' while he's working in town. You wouldn't mind that would you?"

Graeme shook his head. "Naw. He told me he's been needin' some extra help. There's a lot to be done around here."

"Right. I'll be bunkin' here for awhile then."

"Sure. That's all right." He looked at the big man, curious and somewhat awed by Rangi's prowess. "Is it true you baited this pig with a loaf of bread, then leaped out from behind a tree and thumped'm on the head?"

Rangi laughed. "Yeh. I like to hunt. Our people were once very good at it. Only now we've gone all soft and stupid, like the Pakeha." Rangi drew on his Rothman. "Back in the old days we used to eat our enemies," he said. "Now we've moved up in the world, eh? Now we wash their dishes and clean their loos. We used to own land, too — lots of it, not just tiny tracts. Then people like McKenzie came over and took it away from us. Gave us a few handkerchiefs and told us to blow. We can't hunt freely anymore either, because the land is all fenced off, eh? We can't find work, so we go on the dole and sit around sipping tea and eating biscuits. It's a sad thing, mate. A few are fighting back, though. A few have had enough and are doing something about it. You've heard of Pukatea Point?"

"Yeh. That Maori council tried to reclaim the Point, claiming they'd been cheated."

"We were. My family owned part of that land. We were swindled, cheated by a pack of lawyers and bloody land promoters. We organized to get it back. We hired our own lawyers, went before the courts, and were told, in effect, to get stuffed. But the fight hasn't ended. We'll get it back one day."

"There was a man killed on the Point, wasn't there? White bloke?"

"Yeh. Guy named Billings. Hit an old man with a pipe. He paid for it."

"They're still looking for the joker that did it, aren't they?" Graeme asked. "Big man hunt. Covers the whole North Island."

"So I'm told. They'll never catch him though."

Graeme gave up a nervous laugh. "It wasn't you that killed him, was it?"

"No. Not me, mate," Rangi said. "I could never stick a knife in a white man." He laughed, then blinked his eyes, flicked his tongue up and down in rapid succession and let out a guttural cry in the manner of a Maori warrior.

Graeme broke out laughing. "Go on. It ain't as bad as all that."

"No. As long as you don't stir the shit, eh?"

Graeme gazed off at the yellow moon, at the dark outline of the hills, at the Whakahau River flashing in the moonlight as it roared over the igneous rocks and poured its way to the Pacific sea. "I once read somewhere," he said, "that long before the Maori came to these islands, there lived another people called the Morioris, a passive, easy-going lot. When we arrived, we killed them. We ate them and made slaves of their women, and drove the rest from their villages into the mountains to die of hunger and exposure. After that the Pakeha came, and the way I see it, they treated us a lot better than we treated these Moriori people. I reckon when you look at it that way we really can't complain too loudly, can we?"

Rangi stubbed out his cigarette with his hob-nailed boot. He headed back into the house without saying a word.

* * *

"This one's McKenzie's, I think," Graeme said, grabbing the ewe by the scruff on its head and inspecting it. They were standing in the shearing pen in their gumboots, speaking over the bleating of the penned sheep. Rangi was holding the electric shears in one hand, shearing the wool off a ewe that lay sprawled on a pallet, fresh blood striations trickling over the bald, shorn beast as it lay jerking fearfully at their feet.

"Give us it," Rangi said, stretching out his calloused hand.

"No. This one's McKenzie's all right. I'll just drop'r over the fence."

"Naw. Give us it. It's ours now."

Graeme gripped the sheep by its wool and gazed incomprehensibly at Rangi, alarmed by this blunt challenge. "Look," he said. "We can't just take McKenzie's wool. It isn't ours. It's just not done. Okay?"

"She'll be right," Rangi said, and snatched the ewe away from him, dragging it with one hand toward the buzzing shears. "Bugger McKenzie," he said. "The ewe was on your land, eatin' your grass. This wool rightfully belongs to you." He sheared the ewe of its thick coat with deft, smooth swipes.

"There. Now you can drop'r over."

Graeme walked over to the fence, dragging the naked sheep alongside him. As he reached out over the fence to drop the shorn ewe onto McKenzie's paddock, he caught sight of McKenzie's thin, bent frame pulling weeds in his garden, and a pang of guilt and shame, a type hitherto unknown to him, spread like fire up his back and into his brain. McKenzie was staring at him now, but there was nothing he could do but let go of the ewe and stride back to the shed, steeped in the humiliation of his crime. Within minutes, McKenzie came storming into their pen. He stood in the light of the shed door, wild-eyed and trembling, a garden hoe in one hand.

"Oi!" he screamed. "What the blazes you doin' shearin' one of me ewes. Eh? What the bloody hell possessed you to take me wool?"

Graeme stared at McKenzie in a horrified silence. "I … I didn't know until after—"

"The hell we didn't," Rangi said, continuing to shear. "We knew that woolie belonged to you, McKenzie."

"Then why'd you shear it?" yelled the incredulous McKenzie.

"Cuz the wool belongs on this side of the fence. Seems your ewe was eatin' Turoa grass, and it was Turoa grass which grew that coat of wool. Therefore, the wool is Turoa's."

The shearing stopped and it suddenly grew quieter. The tattooed Maori stood up from his stool and turned to face McKenzie.

"You got a problem with us takin' our wool?"

McKenzie drew back. "You rotten bastard!"

"Careful, mate," Rangi said. "That kind of talk ain't very neighborly."

McKenzie cursed, turned and withdrew from the shed, smacking the door with his hoe as he left.

"Damn!" Graeme cried. "You shouldn't have done it. It just wasn't right. He's our neighbor. We help each other out. We have to get along with him. For Christ's sake!"

"Fuck'm," Rangi said. "He's a worm. Let'm squirm like one."

* * *

That Saturday afternoon Graeme and Rangi cut a leg off the cooked boar and headed for the river. They sat on a grassy bank where the water had cut vertically into the slope, forming a pool several feet deep where Graeme often went swimming during the summer months. The water was cool and clear. There wasn't a cloud in the sky; the temperature was mild. They sat on the grass by a poplar tree, attached the boar's leg to a hook on a rope, and tossed it into the stream. Graeme cut some cheese and handed a piece to Rangi.

"Tah," Rangi said. He lay back on the grass, his hands folded behind his head, and chewed his bit of cheese. "Where's your old lady now, mate? She bugger off on ya?"

"In a way. Me mum and dad divorced when I was ten," Graeme said. "She's living in Auckland now with some guy a lot older than her. He must be sixty by now. Runs a petrol station."

"Ever go see her?"

"Yeh. Sometimes I go and spend the weekend with'm. It's weird though, seein' her with this geezer. He's all right I s'pose. Just doesn't do much, you know?"

"Yeh. I know what you mean. I've got relatives like that. Worthless, I mean."

"How old are you, anyway?" Graeme asked.

"Twenty-seven."

"No kiddin'? You seem much older than that. So what about your lot?"

"In Wellington now, though we come from Tauranga. Me mum's got royalty in her blood, so they tell me. She's a princess, in fact, not that it means anything these days."

"A princess, eh? That make you a prince?"

Rangi laughed. "Yeh. I reckon it does. But like I said, that don't mean shit. Only the old folks speak the language now, and they're all dying off left and right. The culture's slowly fading into memory, eh, Tiki?"

"I dunno. Maybe all that's just not relevant anymore."

"No. You're wrong, mate. It is relevant. It's just that not many of us realize it. We're all too busy trying to be white so we can get jobs and get ahead."

"I don't see it that way. Most of the Maori I know aren't anything but themselves. Maybe they've assimilated into the white culture, gone to white schools and all that, but I don't think their characters are by any means white."

Rangi was about to reply but instead sprang to his feet. He grabbed his spear, knelt down by the stream, thrust his three- pronged gig into the water with one hand and brought up a four foot long slimy brown slithering muscle with a set of formidable and intractable jaws attached to one end. The eel, speared an inch behind its monster-like head, constricted and squirmed violently in vain, peristaltic movements.

"Ho-ho! Got ya, ya slimy bastard!" Rangi walked over to the poplar and thrust the spear with the dangling eel deep into the trunk of the poplar tree. They pried open its jaws with a cleaning knife, examined its rows of spiny teeth, and watched it writhe like a serpent against the trunk of the tree.

"Beauty, mate," Graeme said. "She'll feed the lot of us for tea tonight."

"Yeh," Rangi said, smiling. "Should fillet quite nicely, I reckon."

* * *

Jim Rangi and Graeme Turoa awoke the next day at dawn. After wolfing down a breakfast of poached eggs and boiled sausage, they pulled on their boots and headed up the hill, balancing their hand tools on the backs of their necks.

They followed the fence line along a small cow track until the path faded into the scrub and the hill became steep enough to rob them of breath. They had reached the perimeter of the bush, where the nikau palms and large fern trees — with their hairy trunks and broad, prehistorically designed branches — stood entangled with supplejack vine. The air was damp and weighed like wet hands upon their broad shoulders. Graeme stood bare-armed in a black singlet, surveying the trees, a saw in one hand and a slasher in the other. Rangi held an ax over his shoulder. He slid it to the ground, pulled out his packet of Rothman's. "When we finish," he said, "I'd like to have a look around back there." He nodded toward the bush.

"Maybe later," said Graeme. "First let's do some cutting."

"Right-o, mate. Let's do some cutting then."

For five hours they scavenged a patch of hillside, cutting and collecting manuka branches, which they gathered and tied into bundles. These bundles were attached to a metal pole with two pulley-like wheels on either end, a device called a flying fox, that rested on a wire strung high in a branch at the top of the hill and from there downhill to a pole in the paddock near the water tank. The bundle was attached and released on the wire, sent to fly downgrade until it crashed into the pole at the bottom of the hill, releasing its load. The contraption was then pulled back up the hill with a rope for another load of wood. In five hours they had collected enough wood to last half the winter.

Rangi wiped his face with his shirt and stooped to drink with cupped hands from the trickling rivulet that ran by the wire fence dividing McKenzie's property from Turoa's. He wiped his mouth with his sleeve. "This creek," he observed, "veers off downhill and goes onto McKenzie's place. But up here—," he turned to face the dense canopy of subtropical bush, "it runs on your land."

"It's barely a trickle up here," Graeme said, "but it flows pretty steadily at the base of the hill on McKenzie's place. That's why we have to pump our water from a well. Look, I'm going on down. It's smoko time. I put some Cokes in the fridge this morning. They ought to be ice cold by now."

"Yeh. Right. I'm gonna have a look around."

"Right. See ya later."

"Do me a favor," Rangi said, "and send me up a shovel on the flying fox. I might do a bit of diggin' around for some kauri gum. Sometimes you can find spiders and extinct bugs and shit like that inside. Perfectly preserved. Worth a bit of money, if you find something like that." He plopped down on the grass by a gorse bush, rested his arms on his knees, and squinted up into the sun, his cigarette dangling from his grinning lips.

When the shovel arrived Rangi chose a spot by the stream and began trenching. He leveled a small rise that had prevented the stream from flowing into a small depression, excavated the depression even further into the hill, then gathered some stones and mud and grass and made a small earthen dam. Soon the stream came trickling down into the man-made pool, its course now permanently altered. Rangi descended the hill, retrieved a spool of black plastic piping from the tool shed, placed one end into the water tank, then climbed back to the area where he had done his work and shoved the pipe through the dam and into the rising pool of water. When the water crested the top of the dam, Rangi watched it fall, and began trenching along its course, following the natural contour, until it flowed to the base of the hill into a small gully. He washed the mud off his boots and, kicking them off, strode into the house.

Colin Turoa sat at the kitchen table, smoking and reading the Thames Star. He glanced at Rangi over his pair of bifocals and smiled. "How ya goin', mate?"

"G'day, Colin." Rangi stood by the sink, washing his hands. "Listen, since the well pump hasn't been working very well lately, I took the liberty of riggin' up an earthen dam uphill," he said, "which will probably need to be rebuilt with concrete before long. For now I just wanted to see how it would work, eh? So I ran some piping from the dam into the water tank, and it seems to be filling quite well."

Turoa folded his newspaper, the surprise on his face expressing obvious satisfaction with his new hand. "Well, now there's a bit of Kiwi ingenuity for you, eh? Good show, mate. I've been thinkin' of the same thing for a while now. Looks like you've earned yourself a bonus. What say we go to the pub for an ice cold bottle of grog, eh?"

Rangi smiled. "Sounds good, mate, so long as you let me shout for the second round."

Three days later, as the three of them sat quietly at the kitchen table eating stewed lamb and drinking warm beer, there came a loud, persistent knock on the back door.

"Oi!" called a voice. "Come on out, Turoa. I want to talk to ya."

"What the bloody—", Colin Turoa said, standing up.

"Careful, Dad," Graeme said. "He's sounds drunk. You know how he gets when he's drunk."

"Turoa! Come out!" McKenzie called again. "And bring that other black bastard with ya."

Turoa cocked his head slightly to one side, wincing as though he'd been struck in the face. He looked down at his son, who sat stiffly over his bowl of stew. Rangi wrinkled his brow, shooting fierce glances between Colin and Graeme.

"So," Colin said, "now we're black bastards, are we?"

Rangi went to the window and looked out. "He doesn't appear to have a gun," he said.

"Graeme, you stay here. Jim. You come with me."

"Shall I cover ya with the rifle?" Graeme asked.

"No. Let's not jump overboard. We're dealing with a drunk."

Colin burst open the back door and found McKenzie standing near the hangi pit in his gumboots. He had just finished urinating on their lawn and was attempting to zip up his shorts.

"You're drunk, McKenzie. Go home and sleep it off," Colin said. He stood on the back porch with his hands on his wide hips. Rangi stood beside him, his arms folded over his bare chest.

"You!" McKenzie yelled, pointing at Rangi. "I'll bet you're the one that did it." He hunched over and resumed struggling with his zipper.

"What the fuck are you goin' on about, Ian?" Colin said angrily. "And what the fuck are you doin' pissin' on my fuckin' lawn. Eh?" He strode out onto the lawn toward McKenzie.

"Thief! First ya steal me wool. And now ya steal me water. What'll it be next, eh? What else d'ya want?"

"Bloody ingrate," Rangi yelled, following Turoa out onto the lawn. "Colin let's you use his water for years now without asking anything in return. And now, when he needs it for himself, what do you do? Eh? Ya come bangin' on his door at tea time, calling us black bastards and carryin' on like a raving idiot. That water rightfully belongs to Turoa. So bugger off before ya get yourself hurt."

"Ya bloody worthless black Maori piece of Polynesian rubbish," McKenzie said, staggering. "One of these days I'm gonna kill ya. An' I promise it won't be a painless death."

Rangi shook his head and walked over to McKenzie, almost casually. He punched the drunken man in the stomach; McKenzie doubled over, wheezing for breath. The Maori then grasped McKenzie by the back of the neck as though handling a sheep, and thrust the helpless man face first into the mud-filled hangi pit. "There ya go, matey," he said, as though addressing a child. "Sleep it off in there, eh? And we'll check back with ya in the morning."

Graeme, now standing in the doorway, burst into laughter.

"That's enough," Colin said. He shoved Rangi aside, grabbed McKenzie under the arms, and lifted him out of the pit. The mud-faced McKenzie sat slumped on the grass with closed eyes, his legs sprawled apart in front of him. Moaning, he fell to the side and curled up instinctively into a fetal position.

"Leave'm be," Colin said, his face full of pity and disgust. "He won't be causing any more rows for awhile."

* * *

Three weeks later McKenzie found his ram lying dead of a broken neck in his paddock. He called the local cop, Basil Foster, to lodge a formal charge against Rangi and the Turoas. Foster, a short man with a heavy gut and long, bushy side-burns that straddled his cheeks down to his jaw, wandered about the paddock for a while in the sun, uncertain of how to deal with McKenzie. "Look, Ian," he said finally. "I'll talk to Colin about this if you want. But you've no proof it was him that done it, have you? I'd think twice, if I were you, mate, before lodging a formal complaint against a neighbor. It just isn't wise. I mean look at ya. You're out here in the middle of bloody nowhere. Ya need each other. Ya need to rely on one another cuz it's bloody hard goin' it on your own out here. I know. I've done it meself. So, my advise to you is to resolve your differences, whatever they may be, without bringing the law into it. Bury the hatchet, as the Yanks say."

"But damn it, Baz. They've taken me wool, and stolen me water. And now they've killed me ram. Ya call that lovin' your neighbor? Eh?"

"No. But the facts of the case is that ya can't prove to anybody's satisfaction but your own that they did all this, if in fact they really did it, with malice."

McKenzie threw an angry gaze at the policeman. "Cripes, Basil. You're a useless sod, aren't ya? And the worst part of it is, ya get paid for it."

"Now, look here, McKenzie," the officer said, turning red. "I won't have any of that from you. Good day." He sauntered over to his patrol car, pulling on the seat of his pants, which were too small for him. He waved at Rangi, who stood in the front drive, a shovel in hand and a smile on his tattooed face.

* * *

One day McKenzie's house burst into a colossal ball of flame while he was shopping in Thames for hardware supplies. The arson investigators ruled its cause accidental: kerosene fumes had built up in a storage closet near the kitchen. What specifically had set it off was unknown, though not to the mind of Ian McKenzie. This incident was soon followed by what the papers later termed the PORUA BUSHWHACK. It was reported that Rangi had gone hunting alone one day in the bush with Colin Turoa's rifle. Shots rang out, and before long the Maori, Jim Rangi, came striding out of the bush as he had not long before, carrying not a pig on his shoulder but the neighbor of Colin Turoa. The police investigation concluded that McKenzie, who was known to hold a grudge against Rangi, had stalked the Maori in the bush with a pig rifle with the intent of shooting him to death. Rangi testified that he managed to evade McKenzie after McKenzie missed his first shot, and that, after an hour of stalking and shooting at one another, he finally succeeded in "getting 'round back of him". He ordered McKenzie to throw down his weapon; the defeated McKenzie spun around, let out a shrill, warbling, cry and, turning his gun on the Maori, was shot through the heart. So went Rangi's version, which was believed without question by the local authorities.

Rangi became the most talked about man on the Coromandel Peninsula. As the heroic defender in an atrocious ambush and a barehanded killer of wild boar, he secured himself a place in the local lore. He bought McKenzie's farm for thirty-thousand New Zealand dollars, and took out a loan for seventeen-thousand dollars to build a new house. No one could understand how a penniless stranger from the bush could swing such a deal, but no one seemed to care. To the contrary, he was toasted at the Town Hall by the coastal dignitaries, and was recruited by the fire chief, Angus McCall, to join the Porua volunteer fire brigade. The locals, having never much cared for the scurrilous temper of Ian McKenzie, welcomed the big Maori, whose mysterious, fearless deeds conformed well to the provincial ideal of a bold and dangerous woodsman.

Not long after Rangi finished building his house the Turoas began hearing thunderous booms in the hills, deep within the bush. One day they decided to tramp back into the wilderness to investigate. Guided by the sounds of the muffled blasts, they soon found Rangi by an old, abandoned mineshaft that had recently been cleared of vine and gorse. He was standing by the entrance, shoveling tailings into a heap when they arrived. A box of dynamite sticks lay nearby.

"G'day," Rangi said. He was leaning against a dead tree. He took out a cigarette from his shirt pocket, and gazed at them intently as he fumbled for a match.

"What's all this then?" Colin asked.

"Nothin', mate. Just muckin' about," Rangi said.

"Muckin' about, eh?" Colin Turoa walked over to the mine entrance and stuck his head in.

"Yeh. Might get lucky, you know?"

Graeme noticed a pile of rocks that had been arranged on a sheet of plastic by an overturned wheelbarrow. He wandered over to the pile, gazing idly around him, and casually bent down to pick up a sample, as if on impulse. Rangi stiffened, but said nothing.

"Hey, look at this," Graeme said, and tossed a piece of quartzite to his father.

Colin Turoa took the ore in his rough, brown hand and turned it over several times in his palm.

"You know, Rangi," he said quietly, glaring as he spoke at the large, yellowish specks in the crystalline matrix, "if I were the gambling type, I'd wager the family jewels you found this on the day you killed that boar, and that all this business between you and McKenzie had an ulterior purpose behind it."

Rangi thumped the ash from his cigarette. "I never liked gambling," he said. "My father was a gambler. Spent every Saturday at the racetrack. I used to go with'm sometimes and I can tell you: gambling is much too risky. I much prefer a sure thing meself."

Colin frowned, tossed the ore at Rangi's feet.

"Looks to me like you took a hell of a risk with this."

"Maybe I did, Turoa," Rangi said. His tone made it obvious that he held Colin and his son in high esteem, that he valued them as friends and was aware that a moment had come when their friendship would either stand or fall. "All I know for certain," he said, "is that right there in that hole, not a few meters away, God made the most beautiful piece of work you've ever laid eyes on — a bloomin' vein where the old shaft collapsed, streakin' across the wall like a bolt of lightening in a black sky, just sitting there for God knows how many years, waiting for some poor, stupid bastard like me to come stumbling his way into it." He looked beseechingly at Graeme, whose youthful expression of wide-eyed wonder, whose innocent view of the world in which appearance and reality had always seemed to coincide, had, quietly, irrevocably, dissolved. Without saying another word, he and his father turned their backs on the tattooed man and began walking downhill, ignoring the exasperating litany which followed about how the Pakeha had swindled the Maori out of his honor and his land. They had heard it all before; and while the hard, wretched truth of it could never be denied, none of that really seemed to matter anymore.

Tapu

The American stood, his thumb outstretched, on a winding New Zealand coastal road, gazing out across the sun-splashed waters lapping rhythmically onto the rocky shores of the Coromandel Peninsula. His plan was to head further up the coast, to the village of Tapu — "sacred" in the Maori tongue — and head inland to explore the lush, subtropical bush. Already he had traveled to the South Island, seen its stunning Alps, its languid fjords and clean, modern cities. He had made his way north, carefully and strategically, in order to make the most of a journey that he had hoped would unravel the knotted desires for something rare and splendid and pure in both form and essence. He was not exactly sure what he was looking for, an alteration in viewpoint perhaps — experiences to affix meaning and purpose to his life — but he could not say at this stage whether his pilgrimage had introduced any salient changes. Surely, he thought, the accumulation of new experiences was a worthy goal in itself.

Soon he saw an old Volkswagen van come roaring around the bend behind him. It swerved recklessly, avoided a fallen rock in the road and, after grinding a few more gears, came to a squealing halt on the gravelly shoulder of the left hand lane.

"G'day," said the driver in a chesty voice. "Can I give ya a lift?" The man beamed him a friendly smile. His light brown skin was dripping sweat and there were several specks of sawdust in his thick, wiry shock of black hair. The American noted a familiar "Tiki" design tattooed onto his bulging arm — a bug-eyed head with its tongue sticking out and a stubby little body — and recalled the shopkeeper in Wellington telling him it represented a fetus that was supposed to bring good luck.

"Thanks," he said, shrugging off his pack. "I'm heading to Tapu. Maybe do a little tramping in the area."

"That right?" said the Maori. "Well, get in, mate. I'm headed that way meself."

The American slid open the van door, tossed his pack onto the back seat, and slid into the passenger seat. He still was not used to the odd sensation of riding on the opposite side of the road; it was a nagging insecurity, often resulting in nightmares of head-on collisions.

The Maori was glaring at him with wide, curious eyes, an expression typical of the proud, self-reliant Kiwi. Upon learning of his origin the American was usually ribbed by the waggish New Zealander who, as a general rule, playfully despised all things foreign. In awe of American power, yes; but most were universally in contempt of its exercise.

"Yankee, eh?"

"That's right."

"Like it here?"

The American smiled. "You're kidding, right?"

The Maori smiled back. "God you sound funny," he teased. "But I like the way you Yanks talk. Not like us cocky fuck ups."

They laughed.

"Name's Trevor," the Maori said, extending his rough hand.

"Glad to know you, Trevor," the American said, returning the firm shake. "I'm Jason."

Crossing a bridge, they passed through the little village of Wioumu, which consisted mainly of a few small houses that ran as far back as the foot of the hill, and a small general store and petrol station. A man wearing green dress shorts, a black tank top and old scruffy work boots waved to them from outside the store as they passed.

"Hey," exclaimed the Maori. "Why don't you come and stay with us, eh? We live just ten miles up Tapu road."

"Oh, I don't know," said the American with polite uncertainty.

"She'll be right. We're having a few friends over this afternoon for a barbeque. They should all be there by now. I can offer you a spot in the barn and free tucker. What's not to like about that, eh?"

The Maori downshifted gears and threw the American a questioning look. His face, rugged and fierce, seemed somehow mixed with a primitive brusqueness and a smooth, almost political civility. The American remembered reading that the Maoris were once cannibals who tossed dismembered enemies into cooking baskets. It amused him to wonder if this in any way intimidated him.

"Sure. That sounds good," he said. "I'll be more than willing to work for it."

"Great," exclaimed the Maori, beaming a wide, contented smile. "I hope you fancy mutton, but if you don't there'll be plenty of sausage."

The American rubbed his burning eyes and turned his face from the sun. A humid breeze blew back his hair, and as they entered the tiny village of Tapu, with its rustic little store and its drying fire hoses hoisted on a pole next door to Neil's Fish and Chip Shop, he found himself wondering what it would be like to live in such a place.

They drove ten miles up a dirt road, snaking along the green hillsides where large fern grew in abundance, following the contours of a stream whose pools were known to hide freshwater eel. At length they stopped in front of a pale blue one-story house adjoining a vegetable garden and fenced paddocks populated with a handful of sheep. The last of the sun's rays arced over the hills, casting a somnolent shadow into the valley. An old Maori woman was sitting on the front porch, knitting and chatting with two other women. She wore a dark green dress and a seashell necklace; her hair billowed out around her head like a ball of electricity. As he walked past her, the woman stopped knitting and looked at him.

"That's Grandma," Trevor relayed. "She's the witch in our family." He laughed and ushered the American through the front door and into a dark, smoke-filled room full of Maoris sitting in a semi-circle drinking beer and smoking cigarettes as they conversed. The circle suddenly grew quite as he stepped into their midst.

"And who the bloody hell is this then?" a large man in a black singlet undershirt asked. His broad face looked at him menacingly.

"A Yank I found on the road," Trevor replied. "His name is Jason. Here. Give us a bottle of grog, will ya?"

"Crikey. We have an import in our midst," an old Maori man announced, and the circle of friends and family burst into a raucous laughter.

"Yeh," said a man with a tattoo on his face. "I reckon it should be taxed like all the other imports, eh? Fifty quid is the tax for a Yank in these parts, mate."

The American joined in their laughter, protesting that he was hardly worth that amount and that he hoped they would not consider him too much of a burden. He scanned the yellow walls in the living area, and was looking for an exit to avoid all the unwanted scrutiny, when one of the men sitting near him pulled up a chair and commanded him to sit. He was handed a tall bottle of warm beer. "There ya are, boy," the man said, placing his arm around him in the friendly familiarity of a village drunk. "Right as rain now, eh?"

A Maori girl was sitting in a ratty armchair opposite him, quietly staring at him. He could feel her eyes on him as he answered drunken questions about life in the States, and as he cut short glances her way he saw that she was pretty and petite, her dark hair splaying out regally onto her shoulders. Her large breasts bulged outward, pressing against her shirt buttons so tautly that he wondered how she managed to ever fasten them. Her bright eyes seemed to shine like greenstone in the dimly lit room. He smiled at her, once, and gave a slight nod to acknowledge the attention she was giving him; but the girl did not smile back. She continued to stare at him, unabashed, without the slightest self-consciousness. It was as though she were reading him somehow, studying him, absorbing him, communing with him. He found himself gazing back at her, and while the others around them laughed and joked and swore at each other in a loud communal cacophony, they continued to hold each other's gaze, she sitting upright, her mouth moving slightly as though chanting under her breath, her hands in her lap, her legs crossed, her calves shimmering, inviting him to reach out and touch her.

"Aria," said a woman sitting on the couch next to her. "I reckon it's time for a story, girl. Hey, quiet you lot!" she commanded, admonishing the others into silence.

Three men sitting on bar stools by the kitchen looked on, one of them with his arm around his girlfriend. Children playing at the feet of their parents were hushed. The music was turned down. The room grew quiet. All eyes were now on the young woman who sat with her hands in her lap.

"Tell us the story of Hinemoa, Aria," one of the women said.

Aria gave a smile and looked around the room at the occupants who now waited for her to speak.

"Most of you already know this story," she said. "And if you heard me tell it then you know that Hinemoa was an ancestor of ours on Mum's side. She lived on the eastern shores of Lake Rotorua, in Owhata, and was of noble birth. She lived separately from the rest of the tribe in a special house with female attendants, and was so beautiful that all the warriors in the region wanted to marry her. One of her admirers, a young man named Tutanekai, lived on the island of Mokoia, four kilometers away from their village. Whenever the tribal leaders gathered in Owhata to discuss important matters, Tutanekai would always accompany them, and in this way he came to know Hinemoa.

"Little by little, Hinemoa became aware of Tutanekai's interest in her. At first she turned away in shyness, but when she saw how strong and fierce he was, how he danced with the other warriors with such strength, she found that she could not take her eyes off him. When they found themselves in each other's presence, their eyes would lock onto each other, and they would silently gaze at one another, bonding in the unspoken way, with few words ever passing between them.

"Hinemoa's family had begun to notice their daughter's fixation on Tutanekai, and when her father made it known that he did not approve, Hinemoa and Tutanekai determined to keep their growing feelings for each other between themselves.

"When Tutanekai returned home to the island of Mokoia, his desires for her grew stronger with each passing day. Every night he would sit on a hill behind his father's house and play his flute, calling out to her across the lake with his music. From the shores of Rotorua, Hinemoa could hear his songs, and she knew instinctively that the music was his and that he was playing not for his own enjoyment but to console her, to let her know that his spirit was with her. Her longing for him grew as she sat on the lakeshore listening to his distant flute, and soon her tribe, realizing that the music was a call from Tutanekai, became suspicious. Each night they dragged up the canoes and guarded them so that she could not paddle out to the island to be with him.

"One night Hinemoa became desperate and decided she had to see Tutanekai. She went down to the shore as she usually did. She took off her Kiwi-feathered cloak, and strapped three gourds that she had found under each of her arms. She then waded into the cold lake and swam towards Mokoia Island, guided by the sounds of Tutanekai's flute.

After a long and exhausting swim, she at last made it to the island's shore. She walked along the rocky beach, looking for a place to rest, and came upon a warm thermal pool in to which she immersed herself to stop her uncontrollable shivering. She was ashamed that she was without any clothes, and wondered what Tutanekai would think of her for arriving in such a way.

"At this same moment Tutanekai felt thirsty, so he sent his servant to fetch water. The servant passed by the thermal pool where Hinemoa sat resting. He filled his calabash with water from a cold spring nearby.

"'Who is that water for?' she demanded gruffly.

"'This water is for Tutanekai,' the servant told her.

"'Give me that,' she demanded. And the servant obeyed her. She drank from the gourd, and when she was finished she broke it against the rocks. The servant asked why she had done this, but Hinemoa would not answer him.

"The servant returned to Tutanekai and explained what had happened.

"'Go back and get me some water like I asked you to,' Tutanekai yelled.

"Again Hinemoa seized the gourd from the servant and smashed it against the rocks, and again the servant returned to relate the strange incident to his master.

"Tutanekai became furious. He retrieved his *mere* club and stormed down to the shore to kill the fool who dared to insult him in this manner. Hinemoa heard him coming, and hid under a ledge of rock. "Who is that under there?' Tutanekai yelled, and he grabbed Hinemoa by the arm and pulled her out. 'It's me, Hinemoa!' she cried. And the startled Tutanekai took the naked, shivering Hinemoa in his arms, his anger quickly melting into happiness. He covered her with his cloak, took her to his house and warmed her, and they slept together. They were soon married, and over the years had many children. This is the true story of Hinemoa and Tutanekai."

"Good one, Aria!" someone called out.

"Yeh. Nicely told," said another, raising his glass.

"What I want to know," said Trevor, standing in a doorway with his arms crossed, "is how come the girls don't swim naked across the lake to meet up with their men anymore. What's the world come to, eh?"

"That I don't know," said Grandma, "but I reckon we're not past smashing things to get attention."

As the circle of Maori began to chat about other stories and myths they had heard as children — legends that had passed from generation to generation — the American felt Aria's eyes on him once more and he looked steadily back at her, mesmerized by her beauty. The others in the room had noticed their silent exchanges, and were nudging each other and smiling.

"C'mon then, Jason," Trevor said to the American. "Now it's your turn to tell us a story. If we like it we'll have old Colin here give you a *moko*. You'll then be part of our tribe, which means you can hang out with us anytime and listen to all of our old Maori folk tales. You won't be disappointed, mate."

The American laughed, feeling himself amongst friends. As the barbeque was served he told a story of how his great, great grandfather had been captured by the Lakota Sioux and had competed for the affections of the chief's daughter by counting coup on their enemies, the Crow. The story fascinated the Maori, who were intrigued by the concept of a warrior boldly approaching an enemy and tagging him non-violently to obtain *mana* or personal power. When they finished eating, he was adorned with a small *moko* tattoo on his back in celebration of his visit, and he became an honorary member of their tribe.

The following day, as he was preparing his things to leave, Aria presented him with a carved jade necklace, a *koru* orb representing the unfolding of a fern frond, the Maori symbol of spiritual growth and new life.

"Thank you for your generosity, Aria. I won't forget it."

"You're welcome," she said, smiling. "Too bad we didn't have more time to get to know each other."

"Yes. I would have liked that very much. It's such a long way to get here," he observed, stating the obvious that they would never see each other again.

"Maybe that's a good thing in some ways," she suggested.

"Yes, maybe so."

He looked again into her dark green eyes, hesitating before expressing his next thought. "You're a gifted storyteller," he said. "We need good stories to remind us of who we are and what's important."

"Maybe," she replied, pensively. "But we shouldn't put too much stock in those old legends. We remember those days with pride, and some of us become ensnared in our own nostalgia. We get drunk and tell these old tales over and over again, always bragging about how we once communed with the gods and paid tribute to our own kings. But those days are long gone. We need to live in the here and now." She kissed him on the cheek. "*Haere rā*, Jason. That means goodbye."

He said his last farewells, and as he headed inland, passing shorn hillsides dotted with scores of nibbling sheep, he sensed, with a jarring pang he'd never felt before, that something integral was missing in his life — a sense of the primal, the sacred — that which the Maori call Tapu. It was a fleeting sensation, atrophied and forgotten as he immersed himself anew into the exigencies of the so-called modern life.

The Accelerated Man

We arrive on a cold spring day, all of us bussed in from Dunedin. Compton isn't anything like you'd imagine a reeducation facility to be, it being tucked away in the countryside fifty miles from the nearest town, surrounded by paddocks of bleating sheep and framed with the most beautiful views of the Southern Alps you've ever laid eyes on. Idyllic. Serene. Hardly the gloomy environment I'd envisioned. There are checkpoints to be passed through, but there are no gates at Compton — no razor wire, no perambulating guards with shock guns. Just a harmless old man standing in a little guard box by the entrance, dressed in dark blue slacks and short sleeve shirt, waving us onwards towards the garage, saluting the tracking cameras that record our every move. We enter a complex of four-story buildings, each of them outfitted with shiny skins of solar panels, mantled all around with well-tended gardens. There are fountains jetting water high into the air, flagpoles flying strange insignia, polished granite entrances with life-sized sculptures of pagan gods watching entrants pass through metal detectors and revolving glass doors.

"End of the line, mates," says the bus driver, smirking at us in the overhead mirror.

My sentence mandates a nine-month stay at Compton for violation of corporate policies 430265 and 690479. The charges of my employer could not be refuted with any rationality, and so in the end my guilt was declared, my judgment pronounced with all the solemnity of a papal edict — not in the forum of a civil court like in the past, but from an outsourced, binding arbitration panel set up in a corporate conference room, read aloud by a would-be judge in a pin-striped suit who condemned my acts of negligence with puritanical righteousness, all of it sputtered whilst in the presence of my sobbing wife and tone-deaf mum. Off to Compton, they said. Nine months behavioral modification. Have no fear, you'll be good as gold in no time. We have new methods that will completely undo all your counter-productive impulses. And the best part of it is, you won't feel a bloody thing.

Our handler leads us into a large auditorium where a young man dressed in a white linen suit stands at the edge of the stage, waiting for us to be seated. There's me, Jim, George, and Clyde, all of us sentenced for policy offenses. We sit down in the front row — just us and the youth on stage, who looks down on us with stern, paternalistic smiles. He tells us his name. Sterling Birch, he says in a high voice that grates the air with regal affectations. He informs us that it's his job as MD (Managing Director) to ensure we all get the proper treatment so we can return to our employers well adjusted and ready to work. He frowns to make sure we understand the weighty import of his introduction. "Which one of you is Thomas James?" he says.

I raise my hand. He gazes at me judiciously for a moment, then calls out the names of the others, who in turn raise their hands in acknowledgement.

"Right. I have your files here," he says, pulling forth an electronic folder from behind his back. "You, James. Your profile indicates that you are Blue."

"How's that, sir? I didn't follow that last part," I say, openly befuddled.

"No. I suspect you didn't."

"What does that mean?" says the one next to me, the one called Clyde. "What's a Blue, if you don't mind my asking, sir?"

The director launches into a clinical explanation of the psychological underpinnings of the colour pattern that I'd been identified with through testing. There are Blues, Greens, Yellows, and Reds, each with their own tidy, predictable characteristics. "The Blues are dreamers," he says in an instructive tone, "always searching for the meaning of life (he waves his hands about his head to pantomime a man frantically searching for life's meaning). They are existentialists to the nth degree, forever reveling in quandaries, always searching like flagellating pilgrims for their place in the world." He pauses to look us over, one by one, as if to satisfy himself that we are following him. What follows next from this man's gob I'm incapable of comprehending, as it is the most astonishing thing I have ever heard uttered in all my forty years of living.

"Our mission is simple," he continues. "Each of you will be broken down into a cloud of particles and fired into an accelerator. You will be pushed near the speed of light and smashed, your particles reconstituted back to your current physical forms, minus the defects. Our first acceleration begins later today."

The four of us sit passively, horrified by the strange speech of the director.

"What the bloody hell is this place," Jim asks, his voice rattling.

"I'm a free spirit," says Clyde. "I'll be damned if you're going to change that. My soul is my own and can't be tampered with."

The director gives birth to a condescending frown. "I wasn't speaking metaphorically when I talked about the accelerator. The Compton facility sits on top of one of the largest atom smashers in the world."

With this last rather ominous declaration, our orientation session comes to an end. After receiving a handout on our restitution agenda, we're escorted to our rooms, which are not the customary 8 X 10 spaces with a bed, sink, and toilet. They are more like four star hotel rooms, with mini-bars, laser TVs, game consoles, ornate chairs with antimacassar coverings, holographic computer screens, vaporizers, massaging beds, musical instruments, and headsets to listen to any music we wished to call for. We are all on the same block, and to our surprise are left free to roam the halls as we please and enter each other's quarters; our room doors are never locked. There is a small recreation room in the center of the floor with a ping-pong table, snack machines, and a vitamin shot maker. There is no exit from this floor, yet the freedom they give us to meander about makes our stay seem less like imprisonment.

Later that night a piercing siren blares over the intercom. Lights begin flashing in the hallway. As we peer out the cracks of our doors we see a man being lead away by handlers in blue scrubs. He is a young, stocky man with long red hair and an unmistakably Irish face. As he walks past my door, sullen and dejected like a man on his way to the gas chamber, I call out to him. He stops at once and glares at me. The handlers press him forward, but the prisoner stands his ground.

"What's all this commotion about?" I demand to know.

"Tonight's the night," he says. "It's my time to go."

"Go where?" I ask.

"To the smasher," he replies. He looks out ahead as though witnessing the unfurling of one in a million possible future outcomes, then turns to one of the handlers with a grizzled expression. "What do you s'pose he'll give me?" he asks.

"Who are you talking about?" asks one of the handlers.

"The Wizard of fucking Oz, mate. Who else? Do us a favor will you and requisition me a new set of balls. There's a girl named Sheila back at work I'm dying to get my hands on."

This man's cheekiness, delivered with spit and defiance in the face of impending atrocity, trips us all into a fine bit of laughter, but the handlers are not amused: they twist the man's arm behind his back and drag him down the hallway.

The next morning Clyde and I see this man eating a bowl of shredded wheat in the cafeteria. We approach and ask his name.

"I can't seem to remember anything," he tells me, stirring his coffee in endless circles. "They said this might happen — that it would take awhile to recover. I'll let you know who I am in a few days."

"How do you feel? Do you remember anything at all?"

"I feel rejuvenated," he says. "Revitalized. Like I've finally caught up on lost sleep. Like I said, I really can't remember anything, including what happened to me."

"How the bloody hell did they put you back together?" Clyde wonders.

"I don't know," replies the man.

"Do you know anything about who you are?" I press. "Anything at all? Your family? Where you lived? Your job?"

"I only know what they tell me. Evidently I'm a professor from Christchurch. I'm divorced, live alone, and have two kids, but I don't remember their faces or their names. They say I swindled research funds and stashed it overseas. The government sent me here for restitution."

Afterwards we maintain a vigilant look out for the Accelerated Man. We need to know what this smasher has done to him, how it changed him, whether he is missing any parts, how it feels to be transmuted into something inexplicably different. We had not known this man, so we have no idea what these differences amount to and are puzzled that the defect-free soul we'd been told would materialize from the accelerator seems really not so different than your average sod. He is not any more intelligent than any of us. Nor is he any stronger or faster or wittier or more efficient in doing tasks. Now and then we see his handlers taking him to lab rooms for training and reeducation sessions. He looks completely normal, joking sarcastically

New Zealand

like he'd done in the hallway prior to his acceleration. Feeling sorry for him, we take him under our wing, inviting him to our rooms after dinner and turning on the vaporizer (which has a mildly intoxicating effect), watching rugby matches in 3D — hanging out like regular mates so that he'd begin to remember things and become himself again.

One day the handlers let many of us out onto the grounds to take in the sunshine. There is a park of sorts in the back: bright green grass, rows of weeping willows and poplars blowing in a southerly wind, marble obelisks and Greek statues placed along footpaths that wind around Japanese ponds with ducks and geese and egrets. I find the Accelerated Man sitting alone on a bench, gazing out at one of the ponds, a vacant, forlorn look on his face. I sit down beside him and take a deep breath, heaving my chest in and out.

"A lot of ozone today," I say. "We should be wearing our masks."

He looks at me, but does not say anything.

"Do you remember anything yet?" I ask.

"Yes, many things are coming back to me now," he replies. After a short silence, he says, introspectively: "I remember my wife, Annette — and the day we got married in St. Francis Cathedral. I remember when my eldest daughter slammed the car door on her finger. I remember the dry spells when I couldn't write; the nagging self-doubt and the pressure to publish; the drunken brawls and gambling at the track; and watching our bank account dwindle as the debt collectors called, screaming at us to pay up. This morning I remembered having an affair with one of my students, a young beauty from Chile named Ana — how she seduced me with her tantric poetry while laying naked with me in bed, kissing my cheeks repeatedly, in slow motion, with tiny little pecks. I remember the desperation when it all began to crumble and fall apart, the glares of disbelief and disappointment in the faces of my family and

186

the faculty that I worked with — how even my students began to lose faith in me and walk out of my class in disgust, delivering for all to see anonymous skymail notes instructing me to piss off. More than anything, I remember the hollowness I felt inside as I slipped into this dissipated life."

"Damn it. We've got to break out."

"No," he replies. "There's an electronic barrier around the perimeter. You can't break out. It's no bloody use."

"But what purpose does it serve, smashing you into bits and pieces and putting you back together again? I don't understand it. You don't appear to be any different than before. Why do this?"

"I really can't say. Those memories that I told you about, they're all just images in my mind. No feelings arise when I remember those things. I know my name now and much of my past; but at the same time, I don't know who I am anymore or what they plan to do with me."

"Then I'll find out for you," I say, intent on confronting the director to get to the bottom of this.

The Accelerated Man tosses a pebble into the pond, watching in silence as the ripples spread to the other side. "Thanks for your concern," he says, standing up. "But I really don't see any point. We can't control what happens to us anymore."

This fatalism is unnerving. I become agitated, distraught by the uncertainty of what lay ahead of me. As I enter the building the overhead strobe lights flash repeatedly like Paparazzi cameras, my ears now rent by shrieking sirens portending acceleration. The blaring is intolerable; cupping my ears does nothing to quell these stabbing sounds. A group of handlers in blue scrubs are coming straight for me. I shout at them to shut off this maddening noise and release me from this nightmare. There is no escape. My time has come. I turn and see the Accelerated Man staring at me by the door. He waves as they lead me away to turn me into a cloud of particles.

What happens next, I cannot say. The flashing lights, the ethereal vibrations seen by others who have visited the smasher, do not float in my experience. Like them I eventually recover my sense of self. I recall with detachment the events of my past, and while I follow the ebb and flow of time subject to all the gritty vicissitudes of life, I recognize that something irreducible has been sieved from me, winnowed like dust from rolling grains of sand. I feel, ineffably, rejuvenated and renewed; but I no longer dream now when I sleep.

V.
UNITED STATES

The One That Got Away

David pointed to a small braided stream trickling slowly over a bed load of white limestone. Trees lined the banks in thick groves, hiding most of the stream from view. "I'm not sure," he said, "but I think I remember seeing it before."

Robert came crashing out from behind a dead shrub. He glanced at David, then me, then took a seat on a rock beside his pack.

"Let me see the map," I said, and snatched it impatiently from David's hands.

Scanning the brown contours, I concluded we had strayed southwest into an area for which we had no map. The terrain was the same: low hills, trees, creek beds, and grassy plains scattered in between. It all seemed indistinguishable.

"We should have brought another quad," I said. "We're nowhere on here. I think we ought to backtrack our way out instead of making a circle."

David sat down on a boulder and held out his hand for the map. Obviously he wasn't ready to concede so quickly. The whole trip to the wilderness had been his idea; any encroachment upon his self-made authority was not taken lightly. Still, knowing he could think of nothing better, I gave him his moment of contemplation.

Robert dug into the side pocket of his pack and withdrew a Hershey bar. Finding that it had melted, he tossed it on the ground.

"Hey, Stuart, got any more raisins?"

A gust of wind blew back his bangs, revealing a white scar just above his left eyebrow.

"No. I'm all out."

He nodded, then leaned forward to pick up his water bottle.

"What happened to your head?" I asked.

190

"What? The scar?"

I nodded.

"Accident," he said. "A rifle scope kicked me. Felt like a mule kick." He reached into his pack pocket and took out a small bottle of water purification tablets.

"Throw me your bottle. I'll go fill up."

David folded the map. "I don't know about you guys, but I'm going for a bath."

"Screw that," I said. "If we hang around scrubbing our wieners all day we'll end up staying the night. Let's get the water and keep moving."

With an accusing glare, David picked up the bar of chocolate.

"Why did you throw this away?"

Robert frowned. "Don't be such a Boy Scout, David. I was going to pick it up later."

My patience was running low. I looked at Robert, hoping to enlist his support, but got only a noncommittal shrug.

"I can't afford to show up late. I'm in enough trouble with my boss as it is."

"You're too damned security-conscious," David jumped in. "Forget about work. Why the hell you think we came out here?"

A grin crossed Robert's sunburned face. "David Nelson's military maneuvers."

David ignored the rub. "Look," he said. "I'm tired of wearing ties and kissing ass. I need a challenge, man, not drudgery."

"No doubt," Robert said with a nod. "Wiping your ass with a stick is quite a challenge."

"It is for you, Rob," David shot back, only half-jokingly.

Robert didn't reply. In the quiet that followed, I wondered if civilian life had made me soft, complacent, risk averse. Throwing caution to the wind had once been a fascination of mine; it had won me medals and rank while in Iraq. But I learned from this. I learned that going balls out can breed arrogance. And I've seen this kind of hubris turn into some serious delusions.

* * *

David took his toothbrush from his mouth. He spat out the foam, then cupped his hands and dipped them into the stream.

Robert was sitting in the water a few feet away, submerged at chest level. "You know, this really wouldn't be a bad place to camp tonight," he said. "It's kinda peaceful."

I pulled off my shirt and waded in. The water was shallow and cool and relatively clear. Tiny tadpoles flitted about where the current waned. Their movements, sporadic and aimless, seemed almost painful.

"Looks like somebody's been here." Robert held up a tin can riddled with pellet holes. He dipped it into the water, and held it above his head. "All the comforts of home, eh?" When he glanced my way, he took on a serious look. "Hey, Stu. Glad to be back in the good ole USA?"

His question brought forth memories I didn't care to elaborate on. The paranoia of being watched, of being vulnerable, in the cross hairs of some fanatic hell bent on blowing your brains out, was a feeling I'd lived with for two years. I'd lived through three roadside bombs, five rocket-propelled grenades, countless mortars, thousands of bullets. I'd seen it all. Seen my friends full of holes, split into pieces. Seen innocents killed by cross fire and aerial bombardment. I have a picture of myself that I cut out of a magazine. I was lying on the sand holding my leg. A medic is running behind me in the distance, and a young soldier is at my side glaring into the lens. Beside me a small Iraqi boy stands, smiling fearlessly into the camera, as if to say: "*Welcome to Iraq.*"

We were, all of us, naked as the day we were born.

"Yeah. Very glad."

David was staring into the stream. His rugged face looked slightly tired. And when he looked up, having felt my eyes, I knew he didn't want to talk about it either: we did not see eye-to-eye on Iraq, and the inevitable conclusion of any discussion on the subject always boiled down to loyalty to the cause. "How can you question us being over here?" he once asked me. "Don't get sucked into a moral quandary over this. It will just mess with your brain." "Right," I had said in reply. "Ours is not to reason why. Ours is to get shot and die."

Robert dumped a can of water over his head. He wiped his eyes, spat the dripping water from his lips, and stared lazily upstream as though absorbing the green and yellow hues surrounding us. At certain times his Indian blood seemed to creep out, spreading calm over his eyes and solidity to his bearing. He rarely shared these moments of inner harmony, but when he did one felt almost privileged. I remember once overhearing him tell his girlfriend, who had been complaining that he never shared his true feelings with her, that every man has a depth to which he dives alone, and that to openly bare one's soul to others was tantamount to farting in church. Disgusted with his crass metaphysics, she packed her bags and moved out soon afterwards.

Robert's eyes suddenly narrowed. He stood up, threw the bar of soap on the sandy bank next to David, and started walking upstream.

"Hey. Where the hell are you going?"

He pointed. "Look up there, on the left bank. See anything?"

I looked, but saw nothing unusual.

David asked him what it was.

"I'm not sure; it looks like a bucket or something. I wonder if someone lives around here."

"This is a national park. Nobody lives here, unless they're gypsies."

He splashed up the bank and grabbed his shorts and tennis shoes.

"What are you doing?" I asked.

"Well. If there are any gypsies around, maybe they can tell us our future."

"Bring the women back here," David said. "Let them tell us."

When he left, David and I sat on the bank, lost within the privacy of our thoughts. We would glance at each other, sensing the social obligation, but not the desire, to communicate. We looked away, trying hard to act oblivious to the past.

* * *

It was not long before we heard the screams.

I crossed to the left bank and sprinted through the weeds. David was close behind. He was still wearing his shorts and tennis shoes, and before long he took the lead, bounding over rocks and underbrush like an antelope.

When we came to the sand bar where Robert had seen the bucket, we headed into the patch of trees. There was something of a path, a semi-cleared area where the grass had been mashed down. We followed this for not more than a few yards when we saw Robert lying on the ground, near a small stream, where the trees met with a small clearing. He was thrashing and screaming like a madman, his face wrought with agony.

David reached him first. "Hang on, Rob," he called. "We'll have you out in a second."

I looked at Robert's foot. His ankle has been gouged with the sharpened teeth of a bear trap. The teeth had sunk in deeply, holding him helpless within its grip.

"Gimme a hand," David cried, and as I bent down to help him my eye caught a figure about a hundred yards away. He was burly, heavy-set, bearded, grizzly-looking. He stood off to our left, half-crouched, on the edge of a field.

"Look out! That asshole's got a gun."

I threw myself upon the spring. A boom resounded. Shot bit into the tree bark beside us.

"Hurry!" Robert screamed. "He's coming!"

Sirens were blaring inside my head. We couldn't open the jaws fast enough — they kept slipping shut, biting mercilessly into Robert's flesh. "God damn it!" he shrieked. "Get it off! Get it off!" We seemed to be moving so slowly, as though stuck within the prison of some fucked up dream, racing against time, battling for control in a scene where none existed.

"We've almost got it!" David cried. "Just one more—"

Another boom. David flew backwards. I fell by his side.

I got up quickly. My left shoulder was splattered with blood.

The burly man kept coming. He loaded two more shells as he strode toward us.

I cried to David in a voice that seemed like ash. He was rolling back and forth beside Robert, his hands muffling his screams as the redness seeped through his fingers.

Tears streamed down Robert's face. "Get out," he said. "Run."

I looked at him wildly.

"Run, damn it. Run!"

I took hold of his leg, but he jerked himself away and struck me hard in the chest.

Stunned, I looked at him helplessly. I could not move. We did not leave men behind. But I had no means to fight back.

"Run!"

Another blast pelted the trees behind us. I spun around and fled with all the speed I could summon.

I heard a shot halfway back to the swimming hole. Then seconds later, another.

Then silence.

* * *

Upon hearing the last shots, I crossed the stream and cut straight into the woods. The trees were thick enough for me not to be seen. I ran as silently as I could into the dense foliage, crashing through branches, feeling little pain from my wound, just numbness. My entire body was numb, fueled by the adrenaline now rushing through my veins. I moved completely by instinct, though it was not chaotic or confused. I could not explain to myself what had just happened; there was only a strange mix of sadness and anger at the thought of my friend's senseless fate. I had hoped that I would never have to revisit this sordid world of brutality, where men flagrantly ignored both the laws of God and of Man; but now, having been thrust again into violence, I was quietly thankful that I was not a stranger to it.

The sun was neon orange and slipping quickly behind a hill by the time I reached the packs. Clothes were the first to come out, and the first to put on.

Bandages came next. I dumped the contents of David's pack, and sifted through the shirts and underwear until I uncovered the first aid kit.

It was a patchy job. The bandage kept slipping off before I could secure it properly. But in the end it was done, and the pressure helped to stop the bleeding.

Food. I opened a can of tuna, devouring it all in a few bites, then ate a piece of bread and wished I had something to wash it down with.

The Hershey bar was still on the ground where David had dropped it. I picked it up and unwrapped it; the chocolate was still viscous, and I dabbed my fingers into it and pressed it to the tip of my tongue. Good. Sweet. I dug once more into the dark mass, removing a thick glob with two fingers.

The chocolate felt warm against my cheek, so I rubbed it in hard, down to the pores where it would stay. I picked up David's reflector and, using what little light remained, smeared a thin, sticky film over my cheeks and forehead.

Last, I took my Buck knife from the side pocket of my pack and removed it from its sheath. The smooth, tempered blade slide open easily, and locked firmly into place. The curved handle fit snugly in the palm of my hand.

Now I was ready.

* * *

The moon had come out, and the sky, now cloudless, allowed light to wash the area with a soft, silvery hue.

I kept my gaze fixed on a point in the line of trees as I crossed the field. My tennis shoes were still down by the stream, and I decided to get them first, then ditch my heavy hiking boots. The boots were rubbing rhythmically against the blister on my big toe, reminding me of the blisters I used to get on long marches. I ignored the pain, and kept going.

A small fire flickered in a small clearing surrounded by a grove of trees, beyond the small meadow full of neatly aligned rows of what appeared to be marijuana plants. Slowly, carefully, I veered right, circling the meadow, and reached the outer perimeter of the trees. A light moved about inside the tent, and there were two men beside the fire.

One man, whose clothes hung loosely about him like rags, had a long, sharp nose and a handlebar moustache. He sat on an ice chest, his hands on his thighs, his elbows jutting outward. Pots and metal plates lay scattered at his feet. The other man, tall and lanky, had short stringy hair parted down the middle. He paced nervously before the other man, one hand in his pant pocket, the other pointing here and there, as if to emphasize his point.

"It's not too late," the one with the moustache said. "He was half-naked and on foot."

No answer.

"We'll find him."

The lanky one took a cigarette from his shirt pocket and lit it. He drew, exhaled, and said, "What if we don't? He could be anywhere by now."

"There's only one place he's going."

The other man took another drag, and said: "Whitten?"

"Where else?"

"But we don't know that for sure."

"Add it up." He held out a finger. "One — the guy's on foot. From the looks of it they were backpackers. Two — he can't get to Whitten, even if he ran all the way, for another four days. Three — all we have to do is take the truck and head him off. Four — once that's done, we come back here and bury the lot of them."

Nothing more was said, until the burly man appeared from the tent.

"What do you think, man?"

"Just what he told you." A menacing look flashed in the big man's eyes. "Understand?"

The man with the cigarette looked away. "What about the bodies?"

"What about them?"

"Well, where the hell are they? What did you do with them?"

The burly man frowned. "I haven't moved them. And I don't reckon they've got up and walked off, so stop worrying about it." He pointed to the pots and grumbled. "We got to get things cleaned up around here. Get going on those pots, Billy. It's your turn."

Billy — the lanky one — flicked his cigarette into the fire and snatched a dishtowel from a branch. He flung it over his shoulder, then began stacking all the pots and plates in a pile. "That flashlight working?" he asked.

"Hell no. Batteries are long dead. Why don't you run to the store and get some?"

Billy walked away without answering. I watched him as he walked into the field, moving carefully through the garden of swaying weeds, and disappeared into the darkness.

I backed away from the fire. Crouching, I rushed into the field after him, making sure that my movements tracked his own to avoid him hearing me.

When I caught up with Billy he had stopped near the small stream at the site of the killings, and was arranging the pots for washing. His face suddenly appeared in the blaze of a match, horror and fascination riveted in his eyes as he stared at the bodies of my friends on the blood-stained grass. When the match went out, I crept out of the field and into the nearby trees.

He lit another match, and moved off the trail into the woods.

I followed him.

A few seconds later the match went out. He lit another.

I remember the moonlight silhouetting the branches and the faint trickle of the stream nearby. My heart seemed to echo strange, rippling vibrations. My breath became shallow. My hand gripped the knife tightly by my side. I stepped lightly, and was but a few feet behind him when suddenly he stopped. "God help me," I heard him whisper. "This is all fucked up."

I caught only a glimpse, a second, and though I'd seen such sights before it was as if I never had, as if the tolerance I'd given it had imploded into itself, crumbling and caving until nothing remained but a speck of collected disbelief.

I couldn't move.

I couldn't think.

And when the man spun around to see me standing, painted like death itself, his world imploded too. We stood looking at one another, wide-eyed and speechless. I held the knife by my side, open and ready, but I could not move to thrust it. He could not move to lift the shotgun that he still held with one hand, barrel up, by his side. We just stood there, dumbstruck, confounded beyond words, until finally the match burned his fingers and he cried as though they'd been cut off. I remember hearing the gun thump the ground, and the snapping of twigs, and his guttural cries disappearing into the darkness as he ran deeper into the woods to escape me. And I remember that there was nothing to fall back on. God didn't whisper in my ear, nor send angels to steer me from murderous temptations. Jesus didn't hurl me any miracles: I had only an acute awareness that these men had robbed my friends of their lives as senselessly as the lives of my friends had been taken in Iraq. Still, I did not let myself succumb to the primal instincts that had kept me alive during the war. It would not have saved me, but would have wrapped me tighter within the madness of it all. Something decent had remained. Something humane had survived the afflictions of war. I picked the gun up off the ground, strode quietly into camp where the burly man and the man with the moustache sat talking, and heard myself say, dispassionately: "I'm the one that got away."

Rule 21

There are many who attribute the resurgence of dueling to the recent crash of the economy and the devastation this has wreaked on businesses and families. Others augment this assertion with elaborate theories on the probable causes of this regressive behavior. A monogram by A. G. Thompson of Princeton University, for example, proclaims that Modern Man has become mentally unhinged due to gradually increasing levels of stress. The dam has finally burst, a primal id has emerged and now runs amok, dominating the behaviors of otherwise peaceful, law-abiding citizens, driving them towards erratic displays of haughtiness and bravado, culminating in consensual manslaughter on suburban soccer fields, city parks, residential backyards, and foggy country meadows near cemeteries and old churchyards.

In short, it appears that men now crack at the most inconsequential of provocations. Strangers, family members and life-long friends alike will not hesitate to challenge each other to step ten paces from a back-to-back starting point and unflinchingly shoot holes into one other. These theorists would have us believe that our collective unconsciousness has chosen dueling as a means of securing cathartic relief, a stress purge to reset the proper levels of serotonin in the minds of the modern neurotic. The fact that women are almost never affected by the dueling phenomenon is never explained, and so the critics of this theory proclaim it bogus and completely without merit.

A separate school of thought, formulated by a Mr. Jonathan H. Stack of Norfolk, Virginia — whose explanations were attacked in more than one respectable university journal — purports that lawyers and insurance companies have become so brazenly rapacious that civil justice has fallen beyond the reach of the ordinary working man. With little or no recourse, he is compelled to take matters into his own hands and resolve effronteries to personal honor with face-to-face encounters using single shot dueling pistols. Stack's theory, not surprisingly, spawned lawsuits from agitated attorneys whose sense of professional honor had been slighted. Having no money to defend himself, Stack grew desperate; he challenged one of the attorneys to a duel, and was shot in the chest an inch or so above his right nipple. As he bled out onto the ground on a cold hillside in Pennsylvania, his second kneeling beside him with a stern look of remorse, he panted his last few breaths and died, symbolically suggesting to the world that his theory was right after all — that the high cost of civil justice is the taproot of society's trend toward violence and personal combat.

Finally, there is the camp that asserts that the rage of dueling is the inevitable result of global overpopulation, that dueling has been adopted by Nature as a mechanism to control the unending carpet-bombing of the natural world with an ever-expanding film of strip malls, landfills, highways, theme parks and master planned communities. This theory has gained wide acceptance in recent weeks and, similar to the case of Mr. Stack, spurred an intense reaction from competing theorists. The above-referenced A.G. Thomson of Princeton challenged the originator of the overpopulation thesis, Mr. Harold Jackson of Columbia University, to a duel. They met at dawn on the beach at Coney Island. The wind blew fiercely as the dark cloudbanks approached from the east. Jackson was dressed in his usual blue leisure suit and starched white shirt, his red tie flapping wildly in the wind as he steadied his long, bony arms by his side and tried to look calm. It was said that his small mustache and bulbous head with comb-over hairdo reminded the onlookers of Edgar Allen Poe. Thompson, for his part, stood before his challenge with a squat stance and pugnacious determination. He consulted briefly with his entourage, made up mostly of academic cohorts, and when the pacing was underway he unexpectedly spun around and shot the left ear off his opponent. Jackson's dislodged ear landed twenty feet away on the beach. It was retrieved by a sand crab that clamped onto the ear with its giant claw and scurried off into the dunes to devour it.

Sadly, I am able to write with some experience on this subject. It happened when a man named William Shell challenged my cousin, Steven Holt, to a duel, ostensibly because he slept with Shell's wife, who is in fact quite charming and voluptuous, and with whom my cousin did in fact have a seedy affair. Steven implored me to be his second, showing me the note that he had just received: "It has come to my attention that you have slept with my wife, Angela," Shell wrote. "She confessed this to me when I pressed her for an explanation as to her unusual behavior. Having made my wife a whore, you will be punished for it by forfeiting your pathetic life. Meet me on Thursday morning at 6:00 am at Baker Stadium. You will find me on the pitcher's mound. I will bring a brace of pistols. If you do not show up I will hunt you down and crack your head open with a baseball bat. Until then, yours very cordially, William Shell."

My cousin responded to Shell's challenge by calling him an idiot, but agreed, in the end, to meet him on the field of honor.

We arrived at the appointed hour. It was still dark but Shell had thrown the lights on and we found him where he said he would be, on the pitcher's mound. He was dressed in a Yankee's cap and a numbered T-shirt, and wore cleats to match his baseball attire. We found his second, a co-worker of Shell's named Bill Henson, whom I knew and greatly disliked for his snarky boorishness, sitting alone in the bleachers. He ambled down onto the field as we arrived.

"Good morning," Shell announced.

"Good morning," Steven returned.

"Are you familiar with the rules of dueling?"

"No," said my cousin. "It doesn't seem so very complicated to me."

Shell motioned to Henson to step forward. Henson did so and handed us copies of a printed pamphlet entitled "The Code Deullo", written, I later learned, by a cadre of Irish gentlemen in 1777 for the purpose of standardizing the rules of dueling conduct. I will not reproduce the entire contents of this document here, but will set down the first five rules of the Code Deullo to provide for the reader some context and insight into the minds of those who considered dueling important enough to have its own written protocol:

Rule 1. The first offense requires the first apology, though the retort may have been more offensive than the insult. Example: A tells B he is impertinent, etc. B retorts that he lies; yet A must make the first apology because he gave the first offense, and then (after one fire) B may explain away the retort by a subsequent apology.

Rule 2. But if the parties would rather fight on, then after two shots each (but in no case before), B may explain first, and A apologize afterward.

N.B. The above rules apply to all cases of offenses in retort not of stronger class than the example.

Rule 3. If a doubt exists who gave the first offense, the decision rests with the seconds; if they won't decide, or can't agree, the matter must proceed to two shots, or to a hit, if the challenger requires it.

Rule 4. When the lie direct is the first offense, the aggressor must either beg pardon in express terms; exchange two shots previous to apology; or three shots followed up by explanation; or fire on till a severe hit be received by one party or the other.

Rule 5. *As a blow is strictly prohibited under any circumstances among gentlemen, no verbal apology can be received for such an insult. The alternatives, therefore — the offender handing a cane to the injured party, to be used on his own back, at the same time begging pardon; firing on until one or both are disabled; or exchanging three shots, and then asking pardon without proffer of the cane.*

If swords are used, the parties engage until one is well blooded, disabled, or disarmed; or until, after receiving a wound, and blood being drawn, the aggressor begs pardon.

N.B. A disarm is considered the same as a disable. The disarmer may (strictly) break his adversary's sword; but if it be the challenger who is disarmed, it is considered as ungenerous to do so.

In the case the challenged be disarmed and refuses to ask pardon or atone, he must not be killed, as formerly; but the challenger may lay his own sword on the aggressor's shoulder, then break the aggressor's sword and say, "I spare your life!" The challenged can never revive the quarrel — the challenger may.

"This is the stupidest thing I've ever read," I observed, wadding the pamphlet into a tight ball and throwing it back at Henson.

Shell's second was sorely offended by this remark and challenged me to duel. "Luckily I've brought another brace of pistols," he said, giving me a snide little smile. I refused to apologize for calling him a weasel, and merely dug myself into a deeper hole by suggesting they were both certified morons, even going so far as to spit on the ground at their feet. Eventually it was decided that we would all of us fight each other simultaneously, in a four man duel: Shell to face my cousin Steven, and I and Henson, standing at right angles to our principals, facing each other.

Shell suggested we spot our firing positions by having a man on each base of the baseball diamond, our pacing to start at the pitcher's mound, then turning and firing at will once everyone had reached their designated spot. Steven was asked for his preference: he selected first base. By default this put Shell opposite him on third base. I took home plate, which of course put Henson on second base.

The pistols provided were reproductions of the old style dueling pistols, except that they allowed for a single cartridge to be introduced into the chamber rather than the old powder and ball method. We familiarized ourselves with these weapons by cocking and re-cocking them to get a feel for the quickness of the mechanism. Henson gave each of us two cartridges.

"It's not too late," I said, gazing at the bullets in my hand. "We could play a game of pool instead of trying to kill each other." But the challengers would have none of it.

We each took our place on the pitcher's mound, back-to-back, and slowly stepped our way to our designated firing bases. When I reached home plate I turned and aimed my pistol at Henson, who had already arrived at second base. The others arrived at their bases the same moment I did, and we stood for a brief moment, the four of us, with our pistols aimed at each other.

We fired. No one was hit.

Panicked, we cracked open our pistols and loaded another round.

We fired again, almost simultaneously. I heard Henson's bullet hit the stands behind me with a sharp crack against metal.

Steven, myself, and Henson remained on our feet, unharmed; but Shell was down on the red dirt with a bullet in his arm.

As we stood over him and watched him wince in pain, he looking up at us as though not understanding how his life had come to this, I wondered how men had come to consider dueling an acceptable deterrent to incivility, injustice, cruelty, and rudeness. But then I also realized that if men like Pushkin or Hamilton were brave enough to stand in front of an armed adversary and court death in order to right a wrong, then who are we to denounce it? No. We cannot judge these men. We cannot so easily dismiss them as inferior for fighting to protect their sense of self, their place in the world, or the women who loved them. Had I lived in their time I would have gladly acted as their second. But we have none of their flair, their sense of decorum, and regardless of the reason behind the rash of duels that now plagues us, I suspect the victor in such engagements is never truly vindicated or restored.

In the interest of finding some semblance of closure, I fulfilled my obligation as second under Rule 21 of the Code Duello, and requested that we all shake hands and go home to our wives.

Rule 21. *Seconds are bound to attempt reconciliation before the meeting takes place, or after sufficient firing or hits, as specified.*

ABOUT BART BONNER

Bart Bonner lives and works in Austin, Texas. His short stories have appeared in literary reviews based in the United States, Canada, New Zealand, Argentina, and England. The Crater of Orizaba and Other Stories, named a Finalist in the Texas Review Press 2014 George Garrett Fiction Prize Competition, is his first short story collection.

Made in the USA
San Bernardino, CA
26 February 2017